Crumb Hill

tales
from
the
town

a local history compiled by
Ethan Renoe

Copyright 2024 Ethan Renoe
all rights reserved
ISBN 9798218529154

117% of all profits go to rescuing monsters from The Dimension

Contents

"PLEASE HELP ME!" A Foreword by Desmond Poots, who accidentally wandered into Crumb Hill 4

Why are all the headings pink? 8

Welcome to Crumb Hill! 10

The Box 18

A Crumb Hill Love Story 77

C.H.O.D.E. 84

at 1:17 98

William 104

Crime in Crumb 107

STAY INSIDE! 108

22 pieces of advice from the Tonic Woman 136

Crumb Hill Prison 144

The Building 156

Across the Street 186

Crumbdog Millionaire! 190

Yarnfolk of Crumb Hill 200

Crumbclusion 202

"Crumb Hill" in large, pink letters 204

About the Historian 206

"PLEASE HELP ME!!"
Foreword
by Desmond Poots (opposite, foreground)

PLEASE HELP ME! I don't know how I got here.

I was walking through the woods where I have walked a dozen times, but this time was different. I was looking up at the sky as I went, watching the sunlight filter through the early autumn leaves. Suddenly, I looked back down and I was in a strange town called Crumb Hill.

They won't let me leave.

Because I know about the outside world, they think I'm some sort of genius and have named me the Town Poet Laureate and asked me to write the introduction to this book. I don't know why I'm here. I just want to go home.

If you are reading this, can you help me? Find Crumb Hill and come rescue me! I don't want to stay here but they are not letting me leave. They won't even let me walk down the street by myself. I have to be accompanied by this big, furry monster with tentacles. They tell me it came from something called "The Dimension."

They are always talking about The Dimension. I don't understand it. It seems like a place people go when they die, but also monsters live there and often come out to wander around here?

I asked them if it's where people go when they die, and they looked confused. They didn't know what death was. Apparently people don't die here, they just go to The Dimension; carried off to it like Elijah to the heavens.

Also, something weird happens every day at 1:17.

They never specify if it's am or pm, but they don't need to. I think it's both. Strange things happen at that time and I don't even want to explain it all. there is a lot. I don't understand.

And of course, I can only recount what I have seen happen at those times. I don't know the extent of it. But whatever you do, just don't do anything at 1:17. It's best if you're inside. With your eyes closed.

Crumb Hill also has a weird thing about whispering. They always tell me not to whisper. I haven't, but I kind of want to try it sometime when I'm alone and in a room by myself, just to see if they're crazy. But I've been too nervous to try it out still. What if I get sent into The Dimension for whispering? It may or may not be true, but I don't want to try.

This place is terrifying.

If you read this, please send help! Please send someone to Crumb Hill to rescue me! I need to know I'm not going crazy, seeing all these monsters and all the weird rules about whispering and whatever it is that happens at 1:17. Not to mention their weird animals and weird way of growing meat.

I don't even know if they'll let me publish this.
I'm not entirely convinced they all know how to read.

Please help.
Please.

-Desmond Poots, Accidental Guest.

Note from the Editorial team
Re: all the pink.

We are aware of all the pink in this publication, and we are working to fix it as quickly as possible.

We HATE pink.

We detest most color, truth be told. It was not our intention to affront your eyes with so much color, especially pink.

What happened was, our Beasts from The Dimension who do some work around the office here were trying to be helpful and accidentally spilt an entire jug of pink ink into our printing mechanisms. We tried to get it out, but it has thus far been unsuccessful.

The Beasts responsible have been forcibly whispered to, and they have learnt their lesson. Please forgive us for all the pink.

Regretfully,
Alan Yoop, Senior Editor

The man responsible for watching the beasts, being punished.

You are being welcomed by The Girls Opera Of Crumb Hill (GOOCH)!

What an honor!

Every time someone new comes to our town, they welcome them by lining the entry road and singing our town's anthem, "You Can Crumb, but You Can't Leave"!

Come on in to the greatest town on earth! All your dreams will come true here, especially the bad ones!

In yonder Crumb, where time forgot
To take us on its endless trot,
I bade farewell my love and went
To pilgrimage till every cent
In my pocket was spent in haste,
I had to go and sell my face.
And when returned I to the Hill,
My love did scream a sound so shrill,
So ever since I sold my face,
I wander lonely 'round this place.

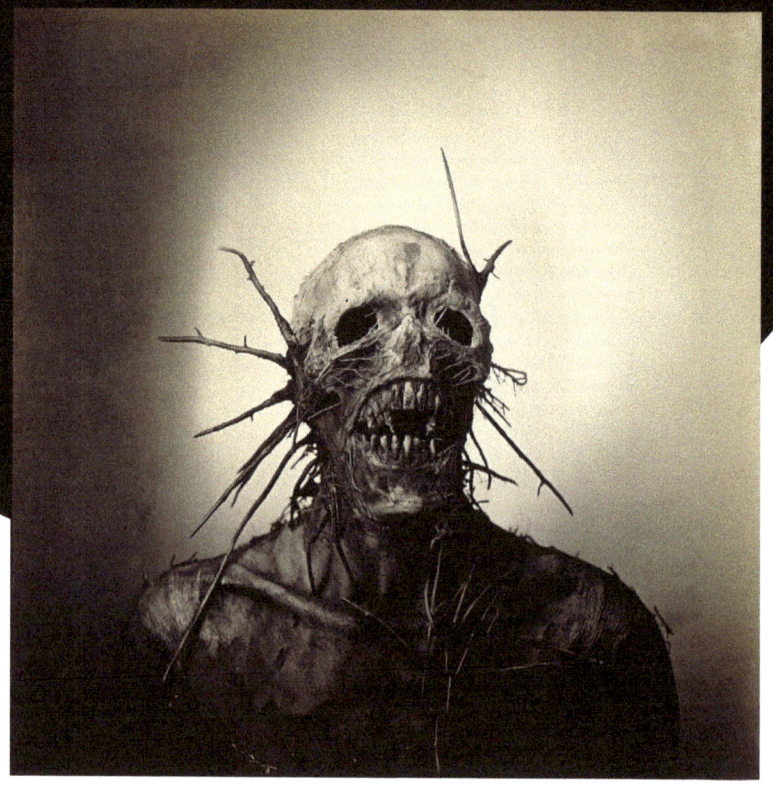

PUBLIC SERVICE ANNOUNCEMENT!

We must remind you not to play with any of the scarecrows in Crumb Hill.

They are not your friends. They do not have your best interests in mind. If they ask you to whisper, do not do it!

We are also sorry for the yellow color. We cannot figure out how to fix it.

"This is Ferit. If you live in the same neighborhood as Ferit, you may have heard him cursing at the crescent moon or yelling at his lattes. His bark is far worse than his bite, as they say, as he has a heart of gold. And I have dibs on it when he passes on because it'll be worth a lot."

Advertisement

NEED A DOCTOR?

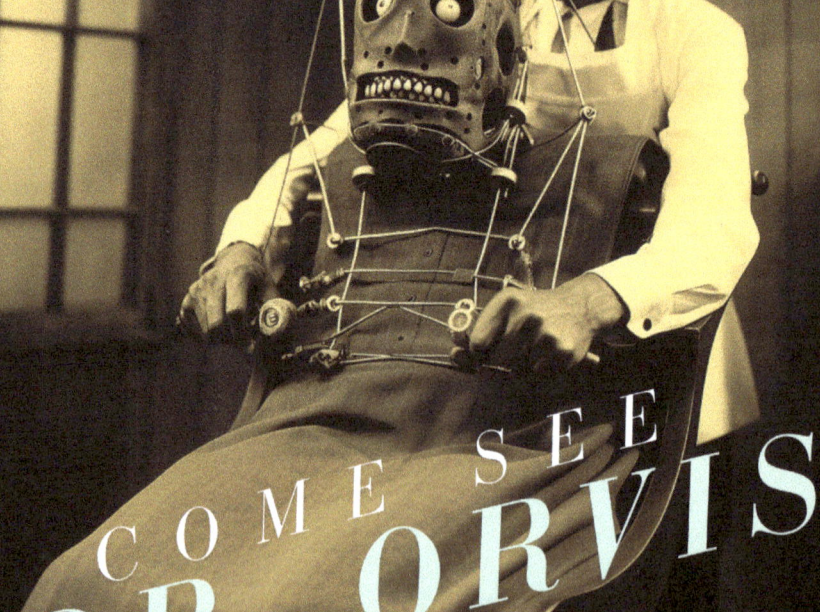

COME SEE DR. ORVIS!

BOOKS ARE OPEN!
Come choose from our big list of fun things to have done to your body! Don't wait until you're sick to come pick out an operation or surgery!

DID YOU KNOW...?

Every Crumbdependence Day (1/17, or 11/7, depending on your time zone), we celebrate the day when all our enemies put their hands up and we won. So, to commemorate, everyone makes a wreath on their door out of fingers and hands. But remember, it's rude to ask where your neighbor harvested their digits!

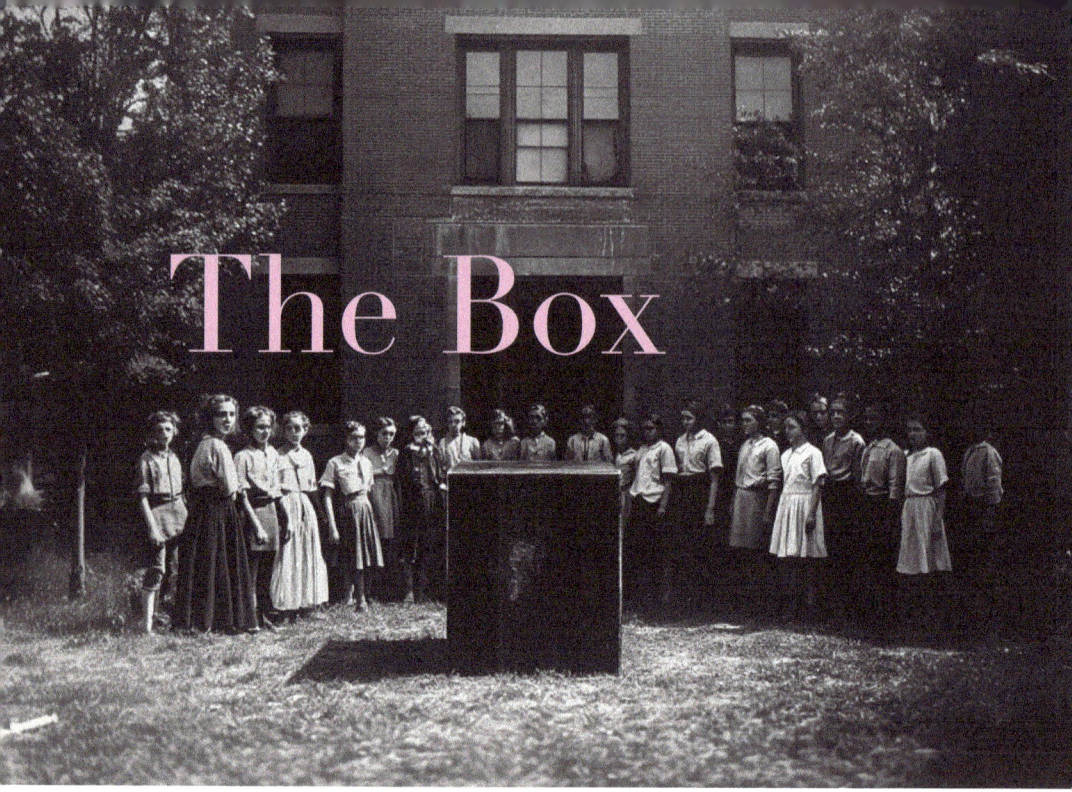

The Box

1

Timmy Shugger went missing the same day the cube appeared on the front lawn of Crumb Hill Elementary School. Well, technically, he never came home that night and the next morning the cube was discovered at the school.

His parents waited and waited for him to come home from his tutoring session, but he never did. Hours after darkness fell, his parents decided to call the police and enlist their help. Timmy had never been late before.

The hunt began and many of their friends and neighbors began wandering the streets of Crumb Hill with no success all night.

The next day, Principal Bearhair was the first to arrive at school and discover the box on the front lawn. It came up to about his chest and appeared to be a perfect cube. It was made of some rock hard, smooth black surface. There were no openings or cracks or creases. It looked like it was formed exactly as it sat there: seamless and solid.

He tapped on it and knocked and couldn't find any clue as to what it was.

After a few minutes, he thought he heard a faint scratching from deep within the box. It was so faint and fast that he thought he had imagined it at first. Just a little clawing at the inside of the box.

Just after the sound, Miss Yarris the third grade teacher arrived and approached the box.

"What is it?" she asked, assuming it was part of some initiative the school was doing.

"I have no idea," he replied, scratching his head. She had never seen Mr. Bearhair puzzled like this — he was normally so confident and assured.

She took her turn examining the box for a moment as more teachers and staff began to arrive. They each took turns walking around the mysterious cube as if *they* could unlock its secret appearance and purpose, but of course no one knew.

Several of them heard the faint scratching from the inside but it was so faint, and no one else reacted, so they didn't bother to point it out.

Students began to arrive and play out the same dance of examination and hypothesizing. After the first few students had lapped the box, Mr. Hairbear called them away from it and decided to put a rope barrier around it just in case it was dangerous.

Very little learning happened that day, due to both events: the disappearance of Timmy and the appearance of the box. Students stared out at the box, trying to figure out what it was, what it meant. Others cried for Timmy. Others daydreamed about being the hero who would find him and bring him home to his grateful parents. Maybe there would even be a reward…

Around the middle of third period, some of the police left the search for Timmy and came to examine the box. They of course had the same response as everyone before them: Look at it, walk around it, knock on it, run their hands across its smooth surface.

One of the cops threw his shoulder into it, trying to move it but the impossibly heavy box didn't budge. He slammed his body weight into it several times, but nothing happened. He heard some scratching from the inside, but looked around and apparently no one else had heard it, so he shook it off.

The police put the rope barrier back up once they determined they couldn't figure out what the box was, and left.

School eventually let out and most families went to aid the search for little Timmy.

No one saw when one side of the box opened up that evening.

2

"Well normally after school, Timmy gets tutored by his teacher," Mrs. Shugger explained to the police the night he disappeared. "He would have left the school building no later than 5, and he normally comes straight home. He'd be here by 5:30 at the latest."

"And it gets dark between 6 and 6:30," police officer Gurt said, almost to himself.

It was half past ten at that point, and no one yet knew about the cube on the school's front lawn. Four police officers stood in the Shuggers' home, taking notes, looking around, and talking to the parents, as well as Timmy's sister, Moona.

Officer Gurt and his partner then went to the home of Miss Yarris, the teacher who was tutoring Timmy. They apologized for waking her up so late at night, asked her about the evening and her session with Timmy, and took notes.

"It was normal!" she said. "We just went over math processes, showing his work, and some reading practice. He ran out the door right at 5, I finished up some things and went out the back door to my car and came home."

"Did Timmy exit out the front door toward the lawn?" asked Gurt.

"Yes, that's the way toward his home. I admit I didn't watch him leave, I was just focused on my last tasks of the day. I'm sorry, officer, I should have paid more attention to him, but he always runs out and gets home safely, so I thought nothing of it."

"That's ok," Gurt replied. "We are just trying to get all the details and find Timmy. You're not in any sort of trouble."

"I really wish I could be of more help, officers. But the last I saw of Timmy he was rushing out the door of my classroom."

"Was anyone else in the building when you left, Miss Yarris?"

"No, I think I was the last one."

They thanked her for her time and left.

In the afternoon of the second day after the box was found, Principal Hairbear was on the phone with the chief of police.

"I don't care about the cost!" he yelled into the phone. "Get this thing off of school property! Destroy it if you have to!"

An hour later, several police officers stood around the cube with axes and hammers. One stepped up and took a swing. It bounced off so fast it nearly bounced right back into the face of the cop. They didn't try a second swing.

An hour after that, after most of the students had cleared out from the building, they had wired dynamite at the base of the cube. It was to the side of it, so it would blow any debris away from the school.

The officers ran to the far side of the building and pressed the charger. They felt the boom and waited for the smoke and falling dirt bits to clear, then went to look at it.

A five-foot hole had been blown into the earth, but the cube did not have a scratch. It now sat slightly tilted toward the hole at its side where the earth had been blown away, with some white streaks painted across it from the nitroglycerin, but it was undamaged.

That night, long after everyone had left, the side of the box opened again.

3

It had been two days since the box appeared and little Timmy Shugger disappeared. The police had gotten nowhere in their search for him; it was as if he had left school and jumped into space without a trace.

Principal Bearhair was frustrated. Both of these events coincided with the school, so it was distracting students from their studies, police were crawling around which was stressing him out, and it was all a bad look on him. Early on the third morning after the cube appeared, he was walking into the school building when he happened to notice something different about the cube.

The day before, the police had tried to blow up the cube which left one side of it white and dusty (though perfectly intact), but out of the corner of his eye, he noticed that that side was no longer white.

He looked at it and noticed that it was black again. But he stared, he squinted his little eyes and it wasn't just black. His pupils could be deceiving him, but it looked like the entire side of the black box was gone, and inside was an even deeper shade of black, like space. It wasn't just a black-colored wall, but a void.

He walked across the lawn to the cube and squinted into the abyss. He stood a few feet away and gazed into it, making sure his eyes were not playing tricks. Principal Hairbear could not make sense of what he was looking at, even as he drew closer to the blackest of boxes and heard a faint scratching sound.

As usual, Miss Yarris was the second one to arrive at school, but this morning when she arrived, no one else was there. Principal Bearhair normally opened up the doors and would be tinkering away in his office when she arrived, but he wasn't there now. Miss Yarris found her key and let herself in the back door.

Slowly the other teachers and staff showed up, but still no principal. It was unusual, and the teachers were murmuring about it to one another in the teacher's lounge. Miss Yarris decided to pick up the lounge phone and call his wife, Mrs. Hairbear.

"Oh yes, he left the same time he always does!" she said through the phone line. Then the meaning behind the question hit her. "Why? …he's not there yet?"

"No, ma'am," said Miss Yarris.

A minute later she hung up. They thought that perhaps Mr. Bearhair was running errands or talking to the police again, and the day went on, though he never showed up to school that day.

According to some who have been there, The Dimension is kind of like a room in your grandmother's house, where the ancient wallpaper is peeling at the corners where the horsehair plaster is crumbling.

It smells like porridge which has sat out for just a hair too long.

It is dark.

Most people who visit The Dimension don't come back, and there are plenty of rumors floating around for why this is as well. Some say that you *could* return, but the madness of The Dimension sets in and you become too surrendered to fits to find the door which brought you there.

Others say that there are beasts worse than any seen in Crumb Hill which will devour, maim, torture, or otherwise keep you from leaving. They will not, however, kill you.

Other people reason that The Dimension is called that, exactly because you change dimensions. It's indescribable. "Ineffable!" according to Terrence Dirk, who has claimed for decades that he went to The Dimension as a boy. Cumb Hill's reporter had a chance to sit down with him and ask about the visit.

"I stumbled down a hole and found myself transformed." Despite repeated inquisitions, Dirk has not revealed the location or nature of this hole.

"I cannot describe it to you. It would be like a three-dimensional being trying to explain our world to a two-dimensional stick figure. You simply cannot believe the transformation.

"I fell into the hole and found myself suddenly indoors. In a hallway of some sort. The doors on either side went on forever. The wallpaper smelled dank and was peeling. I went into the nearest door to me. And this, this is the part I always regret. I wish I had looked around more carefully to decide which door to go in. I think I could have picked a better door.

"I turned the knob and was in my childhood home. But it was different. Something was off. My mother was baking at the stovetop and I was the size of a toddler. I looked up at her, but she was different. Her skin was black as if she had been burnt to a crisp and it fell off in flakes. She turned from the stove toward me, and smiled, a big, rotten grin. Then, before I could even see her move, she had me off the ground and was trying to stuff me into the oven."

When asked how he survived the oven, Dirk is coy with the details. It seems that the oven was yet another portal to another part of The Dimension.

"I felt the heat, but as I warmed up, my shell disintegrated. It wasn't me who was burnt, but the shell which held me back from swimming in the universe's ocean. You know what I mean?"

The reporter did not.

"After the shell burnt away and my crust fell off, I could see The Dimension for what it truly was. My eyes were opened. I looked upon it and–"

At this point in the interview, Terrence Dirk had a stroke which left him in the hospital, unable to speak. So she had to interview other folks who claimed to have visited The Dimension.

Little Jenny Burk's adventure to The Dimension began in Crumb Hill's only elevator, in the Crumb Hill Blank Brothers Building. Jenny, the youngest person to visit The Dimension and return with only one mouth, wandered away from her mother on the first floor and wound up in the elevator. She managed to slide the rusty gate shut behind her and press the button for the fifth floor.

The elevator rose like normal, and it was not until she exited the elevator at the fifth stop that she realized something was different. When she had boarded the elevator it was 10:04am.

Now it was night.

Streaks of light from the window painted lines across the floor and walls. The hustle and bustle of the lively morning had been replaced with a dead silence.

"I stepped off the lift and was really scared. I didn't know where my mom was. I looked down the hallway and saw an old man, so I ran to him and asked for help. But he just stood there. It was like he didn't know I was there, like he couldn't see or hear me at all."

Little Jenny said that she screamed and pleaded for the man to help her, but he walked very slowly down the hallway, completely immune to her presence, even after she tugged on his coat.

She eventually gave up and scurried back to the elevator, where there was now an old woman. Little Jenny asked her for help as well, but only received a blank stare out the open gate. She returned to the first floor and was back in Crumb Hill.

Our reporter thinks that Little Jenny simply went to the Crumb Hill Old Folks Facility (CHOFF) instead.

Regardless of the rumors, when Mr. Bearhair got his feet under him in the pitch blackness, he was sure he was inside The Dimension.

4

By the evening Principal Hairbear went missing, his wife knew something was wrong. He left for work as usual, but then didn't come home by 5.

It was now 7pm and she was beginning to get worried. She called a few of his friends and colleagues and none had seen him all day.

Mr. Bearhair was very punctual and never ran late, and if he did, he would always let her know. Finally, she decided to call the police.

30 minutes later, Officer Gurt stood in her home taking some notes on his pad. "You know, we can't file him as a missing person for 37 hours," explained Officer Gurt. "And since he's an adult, it's a bit of a different situation than with Timmy Shugger. Adults can come and go as they please."

"I know," she replied sullenly, "I'm just worried about my Big Bear."

"Has he said anything to you about this cube on the front lawn of the school? Do you know what it's doing there?"

"All I've heard is him complaining about it being a distraction and ugly. He wants it gone. But no, he doesn't know where it came from. Quite a curious thing!"

"It is indeed, Mrs. Bearhair. Well please let me know if anything changes, and I will do the same."

"Thank you officer," she said as he turned to leave.

Meanwhile, Mr. Bearhair was grappling around in the pitch darkness for something, anything. He could see absolutely nothing. He wondered if he had gone blind.

The air was a comfortable temperature, with a pinch of coolness like the inside of a damp cave on a warm summer day.

The ground below him seemed smooth like the surface of the box, and there was a scratching sound, like someone was on the other side of a wall scratching at it, but he couldn't pinpoint where it came from.

He walked carefully forward, with both arms out in front of him until suddenly he reached a wall. It too was smooth like the ground, and cool like stone. He walked along with his hand on the wall and the other out in front of him.

"Hello?" he decided to call out. No one answered him but the continuous scratching.

Scrrrrch

Scrrrrrrrch

Scrrch scrrrch

He walked a little further and called out again. "Hello? Is anyone there?"

Cold beads of sweat materialized on his forehead, not from the chill of the air, but from the voice that answered him this time.

"Hello?" It was a child's voice, faint and far away. "Is someone there?"

"Timmy??" yelled Mr. Hairbear. "Timmy, is that you?" He hurried his pace with his hand along the wall, and promptly tripped over something on the ground. His left hand which had been outstretched hit the ground first and took the brunt of his body's hefty weight, cracking the joint. An electric fire shot up his arm to the elbow and he cried out a string of expletives. He rolled onto his back and gripped his wrist with his other hand. Blood throbbed in his wrist and the pain grew into a searing hot blossom of agony.

Once he regained enough presence of mind, he pulled himself with his right arm back toward the thing he had tripped over. It was a small box that felt like metal and glass fashioned together. He felt around it with his good hand and realized it was a lantern. His heart sank as he felt around the device and realized he would need matches to light the wick, it was not a new incandescent lantern.

He grasped around on the floor to see if there was anything to light the wick with, and to his surprise, his hand landed on a small cardboard book of matches. With his one good hand, he managed to pry one match loose and press the matchbox against his leg with his injured wrist, just enough to strike the box and illuminate the space around him.

The sudden flare of light burnt his retinas and shocked him after being in such pitch blackness for so long. He jerked his eyes away from the flame and looked around the room around him.

He was in a cavernous room with walls the same smooth black surface as the box, rising as far as he could see in the dim light. He couldn't see the ceiling by the little light of the match. The ground was the same as the walls and went out from him as far as he could see.

Mr. Bearhair got distracted looking around and the flame burned down to his fingertips and he threw the match to the ground, where it burnt out.

He grabbed for the matchbook again and repeated the process. This time, he opened the front of the lantern and held the match to the wick until it took. The flame grew until the lantern was giving off a decent amount of light, throwing a dull yellow illumination just ten feet in front of him.

He held the lantern up with his right hand and continued along the wall again, with his broken left wrist tucked up to his chest.

"Timmy?" he called out. "I'm coming!"

5

After walking for ten more minutes, Principal Bearhair's wrist had stopped hurting. At first he was concerned that he had gone numb or gone into shock, but it legitimately felt better. He examined it by the light of the lantern and moved it around, moved his fingers around, and there was no more pain. He figured it had just been a bad sprain that had stung at first and healed up.

But as he examined it by the light of the burning wick, something looked strange on the skin of his wrist. He looked closely and held the light closer just to be sure. The joint was still swollen, but something beneath the skin was moving around. It looked like some living thing writhing around beneath the surface.

It didn't hurt, but he could certainly now feel the movement. It was the size of a worm, moving around just beneath his skin. As he watched, the skin of his wrist began to tear open. It stung like getting a shot, but it wasn't as bad as the fall had been. Something dark seemed to be poking its way out through his skin. He watched in horror as a snakelike tip made its way out of his wrist.

But it wasn't an animal. As it emerged further, Principal Hairbear could see that it was closer to a plant, like a vine. It made its way out until it was about five inches out of his skin. Then it just kind of remained there, like a plant from the soil.

In terror, Mr. Bearhair put the lantern down quickly with his other hand and grabbed the vinelike plant to yank it out of his arm. But as soon as he tugged on it, he yelped in pain. It felt like pulling out his own hair, if the hair was attached to his bones. Whatever the thing was, it was tougher than a normal plant so he couldn't just rip it off without immense pain.

And whatever it was, it seemed to have healed his sprained wrist in ten minutes. Things in The Dimension were certainly different.

The vine wasn't moving now, it just sat there emerging from his wrist like a normal plant, bedded in his skin.

He picked the lantern up again and continued on. "Timmy?" he yelled.

"Help me!" came the response from further up ahead.

"I'm coming, Timmy!" Mr. Bearhair yelled back. He hurried up his pace and nearly fell off the edge. His foot stepped off into space and he was able to catch himself and stagger backwards just in time.

Just before him, the ground dropped straight down into blackness. Everything in the dimension seemed to be formed in perfect 90 degree corners, and this was no exception. The wall continued along, but the ground went straight down. He looked to his left and couldn't see an end to the edge. It dropped straight down as far as he could see. And Mr. Hairbear couldn't see how far down the drop was. It descended into utter blackness.

"Timmy! Are you down there?" he yelled into the abyss.

"Hello?" came the response from the pit. "Is someone there?" The voice still sounded far away, deep in the void.

Mr. Hairbear started walking along the edge of the pit to see where that would lead him. He had to get down into the pit.

Back in Crumb Hill, the police were taking another look at the black cube in front of the school. Now that two people had gone missing, they wanted to find some clues.

Officer Gurt approached the cube and the first thing he noticed was a small black object in the hole made by the dynamite. He bent down and looked closer and saw that it was a pen sticking out of the dirt. Without touching it, Officer Gurt examined it closely and saw that there were two letter engraved into the clip of the pen: PB.

"Principal Bearhair," he muttered just to himself.

He looked around the hole and the cube and didn't see anything else that would be notable or helpful since the last time. Officer Gurt picked up the pen out of the dirt and went into the school, to the office. He approached the secretary and held up the pen.

"Excuse me, does this pen look familiar to you?"

"Oh yes!" exclaimed the elderly lady. "That is Principal Hairbear's pen! Have you found him?"

"Unfortunately not, ma'am," replied Gurt. "I just picked it up outside the cube out front. It must have fallen out of his pocket when he was examining the cube himself."

"That would be interesting," replied the secretary, "but he always kept it in his inside jacket pocket. I don't know how it would have fallen out unless he took his jacket off, or was bent over or crawling around! I can't picture a dignified man like Principal Bearhair doing that!"

Officer Gurt took a few notes in his pad and thanked her for her time.

The students at Crumb Hill Elementary School had gotten accustomed to the cube by this point and disregarded the rope meant to keep them away from it. It had become a regular hangout for many of them. Some sat up on the top and let their legs dangle down the side, while others sat on the grass and leaned against it.

On the fourth day after its appearance, a handful of students were doing just that: leaning against it, sitting on it, running around it playing tag. One by one, their parents came to pick them up, or students walked themselves home for dinner, until there were just two left: Little Bailee Nuckles and Hildegard Bildagard, who went by Hilly.

Bailee was leaning against the wall of the cube while Hilly paced back and forth in front of her in the grass. They talked about school, homework, boys, food, and everything else while the sun went down beyond the school building. Hilly was saying something about the various boys who had crushes on her while looking at a spot in the grass. When she had finished her statement, Bailee said nothing.

"Well??" she said, looking up from the grass. Then she screamed.

Bailee wasn't there, only her shoes were, with her feet still in them.

6

Hilly kept screaming, staring at the shoed feet of her friend lying there, a foot from the black cube. From inside the school, Miss Yarris heard the screams and ran out to see what the problem was.

She found Hilly there, staring at the cube and screaming hysterically.

"Hilly, what happened?" she asked. "What's wrong?"

Hilly began stuttering, now through sobs. "Bailee was sitting-g th-there," she began, "and I looked away and I look-ked, and she was g-gone."

That's when Miss Yarris saw the shoes. The little girls' shoes had stained the grass around them a dark brown. Otherwise, the cube and the area around it looked the same as ever.

"Come inside Hilly, let's call the police and you should wait for your parents inside," said Miss Yarris, putting her arm around Hilly.

Mr. Bearhair had walked quite a distance along the edge of the drop-off and saw no way to get down. Every now and then, he continued to hear the little voice crying out from down below. "Hello? Is someone there to help me?"

He made a decision to try to climb down. Either he went now, or his lantern would eventually burn out and they would both be back in the blackness.

Mr. Hairbear set the lantern on the ground and lowered himself onto his stomach on the corner of the abyss and spun so his legs dropped off over the blackness. He inched himself backwards, still on his sizeable stomach, and grabbed the lantern. There was no solid plan at this point; he was making it up as he went and hoping for the best.

But as he grabbed the lantern with his right hand, he noticed something strange happening with his left hand, which lay flat on the smooth ground, holding him from sliding into the pit.

The vines which had grown out of his wrist had slowly been multiplying, and now seemed to be alive again. They were moving around like snakes, seeming to sniff along the ground. Each one found the smallest fissure or crack in the ground and dove into it, securing itself to the ground.

Each vine latched itself to the floor as Mr. Bearhair watched in fascination. He almost forgot that half of his body was dangling over a dark cliff, and caught the lantern just before it slipped out of the fingers of his right hand.

As the vines seemed to multiply before his eyes, each finding a new spot to latch onto the floor, they began to extend in length as well. He let himself slide further over the corner and into the darkness, and to his relief, the vines began to lower him down until he was hanging down the side of the ledge by his left hand, with the lantern in his right.

Its rays of light reached out as far as they could into the abyss, but found nothing but more blackness. He could see the smooth black wall along which he was being lowered, and the vines letting him down slowly, and nothing else.

As he continued to descend into the darkness, he yelled, "Timmy, I'm coming!"

Bailee fell backwards into The Dimension.

The wall of the box had opened as she leaned against it and she fell through, but it closed just as quickly, chopping off her feet. But as she fell through light, yellow air, she felt no pain. She didn't even feel afraid.

Bailee simply felt content for the first time in a long time. As she fell for an incredibly long time, she noticed two things. She seemed to be falling slowly, as if gravity was suddenly half as strong. It felt more like she was being lowered through thick, full air to a gentle ground — she had no fear of hitting it.

And the other thing she noticed was what grew out of her ankles. Where her feet once were, now something else was emerging. She couldn't tell what it was, but there were no wounds or blood — something hard was emerging from the ends of her legs.

She hit the ground with a poof, like a pillow being tossed onto a bed.

Bailee sat up and began to take in the surroundings. Her eyes had been fixed on her legs during her fall, so now she could actually look around and see where she was.

Bailee, too, quickly realized that she was not in Crumb Hill, or anywhere she knew before — it must be The Dimension. She was on a grassy hill in an idyllic prairie, only the grass was not green but gold. It wasn't dead though, it was a vibrant sort of gold, as if it had surpassed being green and become more alive and golden. The sky also was a permanent shimmering gold, as if it had gotten stuck in an eternal sunset.

Bailee didn't see any other living things at first, just some gathered trees in random clusters in the distance. The soft, golden grass below her was comfortable like a cushion and she felt at peace.

After taking in her surroundings, she looked back at her feet and was shocked to find that they were being replaced with something else entirely. The skin around her ankles was hardening like a fingernail, with cartilaginous strands. The bottoms were becoming black, thick and dense like a four-inch nail.

The process happened quickly, before her eyes, and she was shocked as she realized what was now growing where her feet used to be.

Bailee spoke it out loud.

"Hooves?"

7

Officer Gurt was getting tired of responding to emergency calls. Not because they weren't real emergencies, but because they *were*. The folks of Crumb Hill were accustomed to weird things happening, but when they got hit, they got hit hard. And three disappearances in one week was rough.

He now stood in the school building again, talking to Miss Yarris and Little Hilly Bildagard. He had gotten there before her parents, or any other authorities, and was listening to the story through Hilly's sobs.

"…and j-just her shoes and f-feet were there," concluded Hilly.

"I see," he replied. "Thank you for sharing that with me. I'm going to go look at the cube again, can you stay here with Miss Yarris and just try to breathe?"

He walked to the cube once again and just as Hilly had said, found the feet lying near the box. He bent down to look at them and it was just as the girl had said. There were two little girl's shoes, with feet inside of them. It looked like a clean cut at the ankles, both at similar, yet slightly different angles.

Officer Gurt looked at the box and still noticed nothing different about it. It looked solid and dead as ever. It just sat there. He wracked his brain trying to piece together Principal Bearhair's pen, and these shoes, and Little Timmy Shugger, and how they all fit together. Or were they not connected at all? He made a few more notes in his pad.

Bailee stared at her ankles as the ends of her legs formed into hooves before her eyes. As she watched the rapid growth of the appendages before her eyes, she did not feel horrified. Instead, she felt an intense sort of curiosity. Perhaps being in this new world had calmed many of her fears and made her feel at peace for the first time in a long time.

The hooves came together and nearly met in the front, leaving a split in the middle. She moved her legs around once the hooves seemed to be done growing, watching her new feet in fascination. Bailee then stood up and jumped around. To her delight, her hooves propelled her further and higher than her feet ever did.

She even found herself giggling as she thrust herself up and through the air. Bailee bounded around and eventually made her way to the nearest cluster of trees, where she would eventually pass away.

Principal Hairbear continued lowering down the vertical wall of the ledge. Minutes had passed and he couldn't tell how far down the side he had gone. It was so dark that he couldn't see the top where he had come from, or the ground below him. He simply hung down from the vines which grew from his wrist and let them slowly lower them downward.

He swung the lantern out to the left, then the right, and hoped to see *anything*. It was just darkness. The yellow glow from his lantern reached out into the black and came back to his eyes empty.

Mr. Bearhair called out again, "Timmy! Are you down there?"

A moment later, the same small voice answered him from far below in the abyss, "Help me!"

He heard the scratching sound again.

It felt like 30 minutes had passed, but it could have been an hour. At last, a floor appeared ten feet beneath Mr. Bearhair's feet.

Then eight feet.

Five

Then his dangling feet slowly came into contact with the floor of the same black color and smooth texture as everything else in The Dimension. Once he could stand up, Mr. Hairbear yelled out again, "Ok, Timmy! I'm here! Where are you?"

"I'm here, help!" responded the voice, but now it seemed to come from above him, maybe ten feet above his head. Mr. Hairbear figured Timmy was trapped on a ledge somewhere up ahead.

The air had changed down here, and he just now noticed the thickness of it, that the air down here was tinged with a foul, rotten scent. He held the lantern up and took a step forward.

He realized that the scent was terrible, and getting worse as he moved forward. He knew Timmy was ahead of him now, and could hear him moving just several yards in front of him.

"Timmy! Where are you?"

"I'm here!"

Now the voice was just beyond the flickering light of his lantern.

Two steps later, Mr. Bearhair saw it.

He saw the claw-like tentacles rising up dozens of feet from the smooth black floor. They were hairy with terrible scum and dandruff falling from them. He suddenly heard the breathing too.

There was no wall or ledge in front of him.

There was no Timmy.

Mr. Bearhair's eyes slowly moved up the tentacles to the grotesque face of The Dimension Beast. He could now hear the raspy breath and couldn't look away from the dead white eyes.

In the same childish, timid voice, the Beast looked at him and said, "Hello."

Mr. Hairbear screamed.

8

Little Timmy Shugger also woke up in The Dimension.

He had been asleep with his brain wrapped in a dark brown sort of fog, and now he awoke and felt different. His eyes blinked open into a new sort of world. Everything he could see was made up of tiny squares. They were all two-dimensional, like multicolored pieces of paper.

Everything was various shades of brown, as they were in Crumb Hill, but the world was nothing but paper-thin squares. He looked down at his own body and found that he, too, had become so thin that he couldn't even see his arm if he turned it to the side.

But nothing twisted or moved organically; it was all operating on 90-degree angles. His thin hands looked like a hundred little squares running around and moving across his skin as he moved them and the light changed. Darker squares meant shadows, and where the light hit them, were lighter squares.

Timmy had never seen anything like it. He looked around himself again and saw the trees and bushes and grasses were all very thin drawings, made of hundreds of squares. The squares were alive, animating everything he could see. If he walked past a tree, it would get thinner and then disappear when he was next to it, like looking down a piece of paper from the side.

None of it made sense to Little Timmy's little brain.

The last thing he remembered before he woke up was the black cube in front of his school. He had rushed out of his tutoring session, but paused when he saw the new addition to the front lawn. Timmy was almost positive this hadn't been there earlier in the day, as he stared out the window of his classroom in boredom.

He had done a lap around the cube, examining its dark black exterior in curiosity. The last thing Timmy remembered was getting close to it and looking in detail at the smooth, hard surface. The blackness of the cube's wall morphed into a brown haze, and it was from this haze that he woke up into this strange new world, where everything was paper thin and made of squares.

He continued adjusting to this weird reality. The sounds were different in The Dimension too. Every step he took made a sharp little *pit* sound, like a shovel hitting hard soil. The wind in the thin trees sounded like it was being blown through a long tube.

Then he made out a different sound blending with the wind: a high, pitchy howl. It sounded like a coyote, or someone crying, if they were on the other end of a long-distance telephone line.

Pit. Pit. Pit.

He kept making his way through the woods, and heard the sound again. Timmy started to run.

Pitpitpitpitpit.

The paper-thin world revealed itself to him in layers, like running past flat sheets of paper as he ran forward. Then, from the film of papery fog in front of him, emerged a towering shadow, twice his height. She moaned again, louder this time, as he was standing feet from her, and Little Timmy Shugger realized he was standing feet from a very tall woman.

Through the strange, cubic fog of The Dimension's air, she seemed to turn and look at him.

Back in Crumb Hill, Officer Gurt was getting worn out. He couldn't wrap his mind around what was happening, where the people had gone, or where the cube had come from.

Of course, The Dimension was on his mind. Everyone in Crumb Hill had their own theories and legends about it. People told stories about The Dimension all the time. It was common knowledge that you couldn't get back from it once you went, but that didn't stop people from claiming to have visited and returned. Everyone had their own rendition of what it was like, and none of them lined up.

There were plenty of entrances to The Dimension around, but none of them looked like this. They had always looked like dark holes to another world, like the vortex made in water as it slithers down a drain. And they didn't last very long. An entrance would open, maybe one or two people would fall into it, and a week later it would close.

How would this solid object with five solid sides (he assumed the bottom was also solid, but had no way of knowing for sure, and as a police officer, *guessing* is not in the job description), lead anyone to The Dimension?

The cube clearly had something to do with the disappearances, and little Hilly's feet lying next to it were now proof. The question was, did any of it have to do with The Dimension or not? And if not, then where in the world did this cube come from? There was no other explanation.

Mrs. Gurt had noticed the wear these cases were having on her husband, and she wanted to help. She wanted her husband back — he had been so preoccupied with work lately that he had barely been home, except to sleep!

She had considered consulting the Tonic Woman who lived on the outskirts of Crumb Hill for help. Many considered her to be a witch, but others claimed she had saved their lives. Some said she made animals aware of their own deaths, while other people claimed that she had cleansed them of their dandruff. There were half as many rumors about her as there were about The Dimension — and that's a lot!

So the day after Little Bailee was removed from her feet, Mrs. Gurt set out to see the Tonic Woman.

Bailee was having fun hopping around the field on her hooves. She could jump higher and farther than she ever could back in Crumb Hill. She was making her way to the crop of trees on the horizon, but would jump to the side and zigzag and then jump backwards, then forward again.

She kept making her way to the trees and having fun doing it.

Bailee didn't know how long it took for her to reach them, but she eventually got to the trees and was grateful for the shade. The air in The Dimension wasn't too hot — just a pleasant, yellow warmth — but hopping around so much had made her work up a sweat.

She hoped there would be some water in the trees and to her delight, there was a little stream there in the middle of them, the trees gathered around it. She was so hot and thirsty, she dropped to all fours to drink straight from the ravine. But when she did, she noticed that her hands were also darker than before. They hit the ground on the bank of the stream and felt nothing.

Bailee expected her fingers to feel the grass and soil beneath them, but instead, it felt the same as her hooved feet did when she was hopping around — there was no sensation, except the setting down of her weigh on her limbs. And as she looked at her hands, she found that they were no longer hands at all, but also black hooves.

Her arms still had some skin, but as she watched, she saw fur growing out of it before her eyes. Her skin was being quickly hidden by this whitish fur.

She shook her head, and with it, shook concerns about her taxonomic state from her mind. Bailee snorted and bent down to lap up some water.

Now, back to the story!

9

The dark form of the woman towered over Little Timmy as he stood frozen in the two-dimensional world.

"H-hello?" he stammered. It sounded like words, but transmitted through beeps and boops, like his vocal cords were electronic.

In response, the woman let out another loud groan that hurt Timmy's papery ears.

"Can you help me? I live in Crumb Hill and I need to get back before dinner." Timmy didn't know that in The Dimension, time moves differently. For him, what had been a few minutes was days in his home town.

The woman stepped closer, and suddenly Timmy could see more of her features, still made of countless brown squares. She leaned over him and brought her face close to his. Then, she reached down and picked him up as if he weighed no more than a leaf. She pulled him up to her bosom and began lumbering through the woods with him cradled in her arm like a baby that weighed nothing.

"Where are you taking me?" asked Little Timmy Shugger.

The woman said nothing, but let out occasional wails as she walked along with him in her arm.

Principal Bearhair screamed as he was chewed by the beast. The lantern fell to the ground and flickered as it lay on its side, eventually burning out and falling dark long after the screams had stopped.

Once again, the only sound was the periodic voice of the beast, which sounded like a little kid, calling out into the darkness:

"Hello? Is someone there? Can you help me?"

To get to the home of the Tonic Woman, Mrs. Gurt had to walk through the main street of Crumb Hill. She walked quickly and tried not to make eye contact with anyone as she went, lest she get held up in conversation.

As she went, she rehearsed what she'd say once she got there. She wanted to come off as confident and not nervous — no stuttering once she was face to face with the enigmatic Tonic Woman!

Hello, I'm wondering if you can lend me any advice regarding the black cube in front of the Crumb Hill Elementary School, or the three disappearances of the three people — no, that's too convoluted…Or the three people who have gone missing?

She muttered this all to herself as she walked.

To get to the woman's house, she had to get to the far side of town, then follow a dirt walking path another mile through the winding woods that bordered all of Crumb Hill. She made it to the path, and the air immediately got cooler. The wind picked up, creating a sort of howl through the branches of the trees. Mrs. Gurt pulled her coat tighter around her frame and continued on. She would *not* shiver or stutter before this mythical Tonic Woman.

Yet that's exactly what she did.

When Mrs. Gurt finally saw the shack in the middle of the woods at the end of the winding dirt road, it had gotten at least five degrees cooler, and the sounds of the wind had picked up, though she didn't feel it blowing at all.

She approached the worn-down little building and knocked on the dilapidated door. It opened immediately, which she was not prepared for.

The woman before her was a head shorter than her and wore all sorts of random things about her body. She had on a black shawl, but attached to it were animal bones, feathers, branches, beaks, and stones. She looked Mrs. Gurt up and down with her one good eye — the other was a solid, pale brown thing, perhaps a stone? Her lips folded in as if they contained only gums.

Mrs. Gurt propelled right into her stuttering opening. "He — Hi. I'm here for. I'm wondering if you know anything about the black cube in the, in the town? By the school? Or the three people who went missing? Can you help us? Er, help me?"

The small woman was silent for a moment, continuing to look Mrs. Gurt up and down. When she spoke, her voice was surprisingly clear and upbeat. "Oh, hello! Well yes, I can tell you whatever you need to know! It will just cost you a ferret and we can peer into the wall hole together."

"A ferret?" replied Mrs. Gurt, caught off guard.

"Well, yes. I do love ferret. It has the richest natural flavor."

Thinking quickly, Mrs. Gurt said, "But it's not the season for ferret right now."

"Oh, it isn't?" said the old lady, looking down.

"But," started Mrs. Gurt, reaching into the bag slung around her shoulder, "I brought you this..." and she pulled out a necklace made of shells from around the shores of Crumb Lake.

"Oh, how lovely!" exclaimed the Tonic Woman. "It's not as good as a ferret, but it'll do." And she accepted the necklace from Mrs. Gurt and brought it promptly up to her mouth, biting off half of the first shell.

"No, it's not — " started Mrs. Gurt, but then stopped. The old woman seemed to be enjoying gumming the shells.

"It's no ferret meat," she said between crunches, with flakes of shell around her lips and gums, "but it's not half bad!" She took another bite as she turned to walk inside and waved Mrs. Gurt to follow her with her other hand.

Mrs. Gurt ducked to follow her inside and wondered what in the world was meant by 'wall hole.' But she didn't have to wait long to find out. The Tonic Woman walked to one of the few spaces in her cluttered little shack where the wall was clear. She stood in front of it, took one last bite of a seashell, and let out a little "mmmm" to herself as she chewed, and set it down.

Then, she pulled her little fist back, and punched a hole right into the wall. The horsehair plaster collapsed from one punch from her surprisingly strong arm, leaving a perfectly round little hole.

"There we have it!" she said, turning to Mrs. Gurt with a smirk.

"Oh, a literal wall hole," she replied, to herself as much as to the Tonic Woman, who was picking up her seashell necklace again for more nibbles.

The small woman then walked up to the hole and put her face into it, muttering some gibberish to herself. She then pulled her face back, saying, "yup, yup. Take a look for yourself."

Mrs. Gurt walked over to the hole, bent down, and could not believe what she saw when she looked into it.

10

As Bailee lapped up water at the stream running between the trees, she felt more refreshed than she'd ever been. She licked her lips after lapping up half a gallon of water and shook her head.

She also noticed — one of her last human thoughts — that she felt more at peace than she ever had before. There was no stress weighing on her, no fear about the future or homework she had to get done. There was simply a nice patch of shade beside some delicious grass for her to lie there and munch on.

Her tail wagged to swat away some flies and she lumbered her hefty body over to a shady patch of grass and settled herself down, being careful not to crush her udders.

Bailee's last thought before the human bits of her passed away once and for all to her bovine impulses took over was, *What a nice, yellow day this is.*

And she lay there beneath the tree enjoying the day and swatting flies away with her tail until she was taken back to Crumb Hill.

Officer Gurt came home in the late afternoon and was confused when his wife wasn't there. He wandered around the house calling out her name, but there was no answer. He began to get concerned immediately. With all the disappearances recently, there was ample cause for alarm. His wife was never gone without leaving a note or letting him know where she'd be.

In a panic, he rushed out toward Crumb Hill Elementary. He hadn't been there for hours, with all the paperwork he'd been doing at the station. His mind was swimming, out of fear and exhaustion, in thoughts of what could have happened to his wife. *Did she get sucked into the black cube too?? Is she in The Dimension??* He imagined running up to the school and seeing his wife's shoes lying next to the cube. He blamed himself for not being more cautious, for not watching after his own wife!

He half walked, half jogged up the road to the school, terrified of what he'd find. The fact that she could have been running a simple errand or doing *anything* else didn't even cross his mind.

Little Timmy was being carried along by the tall woman as she sailed effortlessly through the forest in the strange, two-dimensional world made of squares. As they moved forward, he saw the world revealed to him in layers. As they moved toward a tree, it was like pieces of thin, translucent paper were removed and it became clearer as they got closer. Like a fog made of sheets.

"Where are you taking me?" asked Timmy for the sixth time.

The woman didn't answer. She didn't even seem to hear him or acknowledge his presence, but kept holding him in her arm. Her face looked straight ahead as she lumbered through the trees.

They finally came to a clearing in the trees and he saw a huge expanse, like the ground dropped off. And as they got closer, he saw that it did — they stood on a cliff over a massive chasm. But as he looked down into it, Timmy saw that he couldn't even see the bottom, it simply descended into blackness, one layer at a time.

"What are we doing here?" asked Timmy, no longer expecting a response.

The woman slowed her pace and walked toward the edge of the cliff. The cubic rocks between them and the edge grew fewer and fewer, and soon Timmy was looking straight down into the blackness. His papery heartbeat picked up and he wondered what the woman was going to do. Was she going to jump with him? Was she going to throw him?

He began to get agitated and thrash his body around in her arm. "Put me down! Let me down!"

So she did.

And Little Timmy Shugger dropped onto the edge of the cliff, bounced off of his leg, and tumbled into the abyss.

11

Mrs. Gurt was not anywhere near the cube, as her husband feared.

But she was looking at it…or, through it sort of.

She stared into the hole in the wall of the Tonic Woman's home and her senses couldn't make logical sense of what was happening. As she stared into the wall hole, she saw what appeared to be the inside of the cube, but it went off in six directions, like six different worlds that she saw and experienced all at once. She did not just see in one direction, as all humans do. Instead, it was as if she could see in all six directions simultaneously, as if all six sides of the cube led into different parts of The Dimension.

This must be how flies see, with their hundred eyes, she thought to herself as her reverie began.

In one direction was a roaring flame. In another was a silent and infinite number of stars, drifting forever. There was an extraterrestrial planet and buildings unlike anything she'd seen before. She saw a child floating through space and was immediately convinced that it was one of the children who had gone missing from Crumb Hill years before.

Two of the walls of the cube were simply solid colors she had never seen before, like a cloud or a solid wall of fog filled the void.

In another direction was the yellow, idyllic fields Bailee had seen, with a cow lying peacefully beneath a clump of trees.

One direction looked like a sleek black maze of cubic directions and ledges and terribly high walls. She saw a beast wandering in the pit of one of these massive, dark vaults.

The last way seemed to be a world where everything was made of paper; everything was paper thin, and made of small, shaded brown paper-thin squares. There were simply layers and layers of two-dimensional trees and paths and beasts and everything, but it was all paper thin. She saw a bird fly by and at one point, when it flew by her at just the right angle, it was just a thin line. She saw a woman carrying a little boy to the edge of a cliff.

Officer Gurt was out of breath when he made it to the school's front lawn. He didn't see his wife, so he frantically looked around the building and the cube, then ran around the building again. The exhaustion from the cases had really taken its toll on his mental state.

His second time around the building, he came back to the cube, looking for any trace of his wife. He called out her name, but there was no response. He didn't know if he should feel relieved or more afraid that she wasn't here either. Had the cube sucked her in too?

He dropped onto the grass a few feet from the cube to catch his breath.

Mrs. Gurt's senses became overloaded and she pulled her head back from the wall hole.

"What is that??" she exclaimed. "Is that The Dimension?"

"Oh, yes," replied the Tonic Woman. "Well, parts of it. The Dimension cannot be fully comprehended or explained. And everyone experiences it differently. If you went into it, your experience would be unlike any of those!"

Mrs. Gurt was still confused as to why the old woman looked so scary and esoteric, yet spoke with such a joyful lightness. It threw her off.

"So are the missing people in there?" she asked.

"Oh, yes! You saw them all."

"I did?? The girl floating through space looked nothing like Little Bailee Nuckles, and she had both her feet!"

"You're right! That was not Bailee. But as for the others, remember that things change in The Dimension."

"So, can we bring them back? Principal Hairbear, Bailee, and Little Timmy Shugger?"

The old woman thought about this while chewing on another seashell from the necklace. "It won't be easy…but we can."

But she was wrong.

Little Timmy fell into the blackness for a long time.

After what seemed like hours of falling through blackness — or was it minutes? — he hit the bottom. It was painless.

His thin body lay completely flat on a dark surface, but he could not move. He tried to move an arm, or even a finger, and not a thing budged. It was like he was being held down by a monstrous weight pressing down on him, though it didn't hurt.

12

"I'm going to have to whisper," said the Tonic Woman. This sentence alone sent shivers down the spine of Mrs. Gurt. Whispering had been outlawed in Crumb Hill since long before the Great Crumb Wars, and everyone knew why: You'd either summon beasts from The Dimension, get sent into it, or something worse altogether.

"You…you are?" asked Mrs. Gurt. "Is there no other way?"

"Unfortunately not. But don't worry! If I do it correctly, nothing will go wrong! I've done this a number of times before. And that number is four. And only one of those times was dangerous."

"Alright, so what will we have to do?"

The old woman walked over to a chest in the corner of the room and began rummaging through it. She pulled out a long thread and then cut it into three arm-length strands. The Tonic Woman tied each one above windows on three walls of the room — one faced east, one west, and one north.

"So," she began to explain, "now we wait. The wind will tell us when the time is right. Once all three threads are blowing in, that means that the three winds are allowing us to whisper the names of the departed."

Mrs. Gurt thought the old woman was crazy. Of course, wind can only blow in one direction, so one or two would blow in and the others would blow out.

Ten minutes later, a breeze blew from the east, but the western thread flapped out the window.

The Tonic Woman looked at Mrs. Gurt and smiled. She could tell that the younger woman thought she was crazy, and said, "Patience."

It was almost an hour before all three threads were blowing in from their respective windows. A steady breeze came from three directions, blowing all three strings in to about a 45 degree angle between the ceiling and the wall.

"It's time!" The older woman hopped up and hurried over to the wall hole. She put her face into it, and Mrs. Gurt barely heard her whisper into it.

"Little Timmy Shugger," she clearly annunciated through a whisper into the hole, with her face pressed all the way into it. "Principal Bearhair. Little Bailee Nuckles."

She then pulled her face out of the hole and immediately the wind died down. Mrs. Gurt had been tense the entire time, expecting something terrible to come from the whispering. She waited, and looked around, out the windows, watching for a monster. But nothing came. She allowed her body to relax and she finally inhaled.

"It worked?" she asked the Tonic Woman.

"I think so," said the older woman, taking another bite of seashell.

"Well, that was easy."

"Yup, sometimes I'm wrong about things!" replied the Tonic Woman with bits of seashell sputtering from her lips.

After thanking her for her time, Mrs. Gurt walked back to town. She realized it had gotten late and her husband may be worried about her.

But after arriving at their home and finding it empty, she decided to walk to the school, out of curiosity.

The sun was dropping beneath the horizon as Officer Gurt sat next to the cube. Suddenly, he heard moaning coming from it. He hopped up to his feet and ran to it, then around it.

"Hello??" he yelled at the smooth walls of the black box.

The moaning continued. It sounded like it was coming from under the thing. Officer Gurt ran around to the side where the dynamite had blown a hole in the ground beneath it. He began pulling dirt out from under it with his hands.

The cries sounded like a child stuck under the cube.

"Hello?" he yelled again while pulling out clumps of dirt. "I'll get you out!"

Officer Gurt heard footsteps behind him as he was digging, his face down in the hole. Without turning to look, he yelled, "Hey! Get help! Or help me dig! I think someone is under the cube!"

When there was no response, Officer Gurt looked over his shoulder and saw a cow standing near him, eating some grass from the lawn. He was so jarred that he paused and stared at it for a moment.

Must have escaped from someone's farm.

He turned back and continued digging.

Half an hour later, his wife approached the school and found her husband halfway beneath the cube, his legs sticking out into the hole. A cow was chewing on the lawn some thirty feet from the cube.

"Honey?" she said as she approached. "Is that you?"

"Just....about..." he said from beneath the box, out of breath. "Got it!"

She watched as his feet scooted backward out from under the box and he emerged from the hole. Then Mrs. Gurt was shocked to see a child-sized piece of paper follow him out of the hole. It was the size of a little boy, like a moving, living sheet. It was paper thin, but moved like a kid.

When it turned to face her and she could see it fully from the front, she exclaimed, "Little Timmy Shugger!"

A week later, Bailee still had not been found.

After digging Little Timmy out from under the cube, they had discovered a bunch of chewed up pieces of someone lying nearby. Since people don't die in Crumb Hill — they just go to The Dimension when they're too old to shovel — the bits of the person were still alive. After some investigation, the police determined the mushy pieces were Principal Bearhair.

Doctors are still trying to piece him back together, but they have made one thing clear: "Don't expect him to dance a Jittercrumb anytime soon; his spleen and left tibia would slide right out."

No one knew who the cow belonged to. No farmers were missing any of theirs, so the residents of Crumb Hill just let her wander freely around the town, and she quickly became a sort of well-known fixture around the town. The people began to affectionately refer to her as Bailee, since she had mysteriously appeared the same way Little Bailey had mysteriously disappeared.

Little Timmy never went back to his normal dimensions. He is still two-dimensional, and doctors think that he may always be. They have to use hammers to smash his food down to a digestible proportion and then slide the thin food into his mouth.

And the cube disappeared the day after Little Timmy returned. There was a square patch of yellow grass in front of the school next to a big hole in the earth. It was determined that it was simply the most unique entrance to The Dimension that had opened in the town yet, and they'd be more careful with mysterious objects in the future.

the end

[CAPTION REDACTED]

FUN FACT!

In Crumb Hill, height is measured from the ground to the chin, not the top of the head. This is because residents believe the face "doesn't count."

A Crumb Hill Love Story

He had loved her for a long time. It seemed that he loved her more every day—something he hadn't thought possible—now that he was becoming translucent.

His body, not as opaque as it once was, still enjoyed going on walks with her through the gardens and throughout Crumb Forest.

When they were young and the world was brighter to their eyes, Crumb Hill seemed so full of potential and life. They blinked and before they knew it, they'd grown old together.

Well, she had grown older.

But instead of aging and sagging and balding, he had become more transparent. Soon there would be none of him left to look at, just a warm impression on their bed or the slight breeze of the door cracking open.

They both knew that day would come but it was not here yet. So they hold onto the days they do have together, both visible and ambulatory.

She enjoys the cool evening wind on her skin and he even likes the way it feels blowing through him.

They hold and behold one another while they still can.

Love in Crumb Hill can be a funny thing.

Del Whorgle wants to remind everyone that "THERE ARE NO PEOPLE IN MY BAKED GOODS! They just scream sometimes because of the yeast I use. Please stop saying there are people in them."

These guys answered the door for The Swarm and suddenly they're just visitors at their own (former) home!

But really, if The Swarm knocks on your door, DO. NOT. ANSWER. IT.

They will kick you out and tie you up with so much legal litigation it may as well have never been yours. Please watch out for The Swarm.

"I keep having the strangest dream. It's 1:17 and the One We Can't Pronounce is drawing closer to us."

"It lives in Crumb Lake and we need to feed it every week or else it will wake up."

Divers also descend into the depths of the lake to beat up the fish to remind them to stay in the water, where they belong. This is what we in Crumb Hill call "Fishing." We all recall what happened the last week the fish weren't whooped.

"We were children dreaming about love in some disembodied sort of way until we grew up and acted it out."

"Our love is a realized thing; we choose one another every day. It's no longer a theory, love is a bad-breath, grumpy-morning kind of reality."

Mary-Louise and Elfred, as children, and on the day of their wedding. We just love a good story of a couple who have been friends since childhood and tie the knot! We do hope, for everyone's safety, that they can figure out how to untie it before Thursday.

"Come along now,
 it's time to go to
  The Dimension."

The Crumb Hill Office of Divine Epiphany
an introduction to CHODE

There is only one thing you need to know about The Crumb Hill Office of Divine Epiphany. Alright, there are two. Maybe three. Actually, we have counted and there are roughly fourteen things you need to know about CHODE.

So let's get started with the origins.

Upon the discovery of The Dimension shortly after the Great Crumb Wars, we in Crumb Hill became aware not only of its power, but its diversity, its awe-inspiring range of experiences and creatures and versions of existence. It's another world, another universe, another reality. It's as rich as it is terrifying.

We came to fear The Dimension as much as we were drawn to it with a furious curiosity, like when you stand on a high cliff and feel the pull to jump as much as you fear the fall.

Our whole town became obsessed with the entrances that would open up periodically around town. We threw our cats into them.

This ritual became systematized and eventually people took up the roles of intermediaries between The Dimension and Crumb

Hill. This group eventually became officiated and recognized as a pillar of central importance to the town. It was dubbed the Crumb Hill Office of Divine Epiphany, as it concerned itself chiefly with these otherworldly revelations, both the beasts of The Dimension, and The Dimension itself. They performed the sacramental and sacerdotal duties between the worlds.

The Office began producing iconography on its walls and doors which attempted to represent things witnessed or described in The Dimension. Of course, like Bishop Blag once said, attempting to describe the bowels of The Dimension to those outside is like trying to describe the steam engine or the printing press to a caveman.

Various orders of the CHODE. Guess which one is holiest!

But not everything is left to speculation when it comes to the contents of The Dimension.

Many years ago, there were rumors circulating about a child born from The Dimension, but into this world. The first ones to hear about this kid were field workers out in Crumb Field. A bunch of songbirds came and sang to them, telling them that a special kid was about to pop into Crumb Hill.

So they came back into town and began to search around for this special kid the birds had told them about.

Around the same time, there were philosophers from a few villages over who saw a giant star descending from the sky.

"This cannot be ignored!" they said to one another, and they too began to walk toward the star, which over several days of traipsing, led them into the township of Crumb Hill.

Not everyone was as happy about the coming of the Kid, though. The mayor of Crumb Hill at the time was a cross man named Tommy Tuggs. He was self appointed and liked no one but himself. He loved finger soups and hated wood.

Tuggs had heard that there was a Kid who would be born, and people were more excited about this Kid coming into the town —from The Dimension and from Crumb Hill—than they were about him being their mayor. And this really bothered him.

So he decided that all kids in Crumb Hill, born between the penultimate month of the year and the last month of the age, should be fed to some beasts from The Dimension he kept as pets. So this is what he did; he rounded them up and filled the tummies of the beasts until they nearly popped!

Just before this happened to him though, The Kid was saved.

Two beasts overheard what the mayor was up to as they hung around in the alley behind the mayor's office and heard things. One came and told Joté that he would be the father of the Kid, and that Mayor Tuggs would be after him. The other went to

Joté's girlf, Malp, and told her the same thing.

So Joté and Malp had to go into hiding so they didn't get found by Mayor Tuggs. They wandered out into the distant reaches of Crumb Hill to a farm in the middle of nowhere. They were taken in by a kind farmer named William, who let them camp out in his barn, with the creatures.

It was here that the Kid was born, in a shoddy barn among the beasts. Shortly after, the field workers and later the philosophers came and found the couple with their baby kid.

They found the Kid and this gathering of divergent folks became known as the Natiblity. Little did they know that their likenesses would be rendered countless times in Crumb homes as they reflected back on the first Kristerkin, otherwise known as Crumbmas. (The terms are interchangeable, though some in Crumb Hill lately have been protesting 'Kristerkin,' as they say "The Dimension should be left out of the holidays.")

So this tradition has been remembered every year in Crumb Hill. Gifts are exchanged to remember the generous way that The Kid came all the way from The Dimension to Crumb Hill and taught us how to navigate that barrier between the two.

Another character emerged from the decades of tradition: Saint Barth. He's like an inverse version of The Kid— according to legend, he jumped *into* The Dimension and scared the crap out of the beasts within. So for that, the kids love him.

But if you whisper, he will still most definitely get ya.

Other big Crumbmas traditions include the summoning and subsequent beholding of The Drog. On Kristers Eve, the townsfolk go outside the city limits to behold the Drog.

Then, when Kristerkin is almost over, just before midnight, you'll get a kiss from the Kristergoose! (Unless you whispered this year.)

We love to sing Crumbmas carols like *O Crumb All ye Faithful*, and everyone loves to show off their favorite Kristerkin gifts!

"My favorite Kristerkin gift this year was my very own Little Mitchel. He just keeps chaining up my hands while I sleep."

Anyway, after Joté and Malp returned from hiding, the Kid grew in wisdom and stature and became a man. He taught many people many incredibly wise things, and amassed a following of people and creatures alike. Everyone liked to listen to him.

Once he was a man, the Kid subjected himself to The Dusting. In a symbolic gesture of humility, The Kid was covered in dust.

After he was dusted, his teaching and purpose really began to pick up. He taught a lot, but once again, not everyone was pleased by it. He began to say things like, "I am The Dimension," and, "No one knows The Dimension except he who has come from it and returned."

So enough people came together to form what could be considered a 'mob,' and they got angry. They rallied around the Kid and his followers, and pulled him away. They beat him and tossed Him into The Dimension.

His followers thought this great epoch of teaching, leadership, and hope was over. For two days, anyway…

But on the third day, he returned from The Dimension — only larger — and was witnessed by many.

Their hope returned!

The Dimension no longer had the last word; The Kid did!

But now we've gotten distracted. We got off track from the back story of CHODE! Oh well, you'll learn more about it and the Kid next time, or when you come to visit!

If you drop by the Crumb Hill Office of Divine Epiphany, you will definitely be inspired to change your life, but we aren't sure which way!

At seventeen after one
every day in Crumb Hill,
we can't quite describe it,
but the air starts to chill.

The trees come alive
and the dolls turn to clowns.
The trains just won't run,
and the shadows make sounds.

At 1:17
we don't know what to do,
we've thought about leaving but
don't know where to.

There's a force come alive
here at 1:17,
it doesn't want us to stay,
but it won't let us leave.

So at least once a day,
when that time is just right,
Crumb Hill gets real strange —
so best to stay out of sight.

PUBLIC SERVICE ANNOUNCEMENT!

Also do not feed the scarecrows. It upsets their tummies and we do NOT want that again.

You remember what happened last time…

"Grobble grobble groom,
my sister got stuck in her room.
Bindle bindle boon,
we hope she shrinks down soon."

This morning we found two men standing in the woods. They are currently being held and 'interrogated' and will not be released. We will let you know what we get out of them. Please let us know questions you'd like us to ask them, or information we should extract.

This creature from The Dimension gave a guest lecture to our elementary schoolers on the value of molting (it's normal; everyone goes through it), and the glory of having an exoskeleton.

He concluded by telling them to "work on it," and we weren't sure what that means.

"Some mornings are harder than others. Some mornings I can barely crawl out of bed because I'm thinking about the vast disparity between how I thought my life would turn out and how it is.

Look at this. I'm nearly 117 and can barely walk. More aches and pains. More funerals for my dreams and I suppose this here is the eulogy. Anyways, thanks for stopping by and listening."

—William

PUBLIC SERVICE ANNOUNCEMENT!

Yes, another one already. Get over it. Stop asking us to 'cool it' on the Public Service Announcements.

Anyway, the children in Crumb Hill have stopped talking and started 'arranging themselves.' If anyone knows anything about this, please call 117.

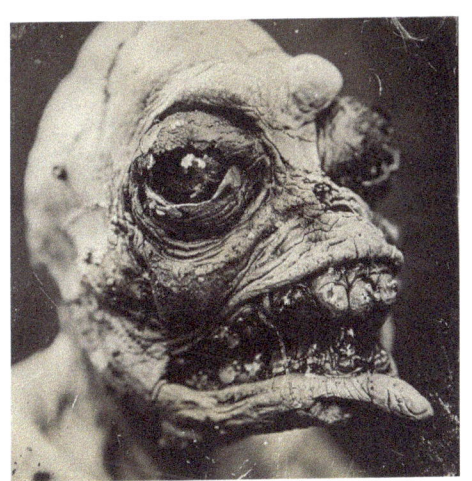

CRIME IN CRUMB

Three bank robbers wore these five masks to rob First Bank of Crumb Hill this morning. Don't ask how three people wore five masks, just use your imagination. Let us know if you see them.

STAY INSIDE!

1

Officer Gurt woke up with the sun as he typically did. He looked for a moment at his wife lying next to him and swung his feet over the edge of the bed and into their slippers. After starting the stove to boil water for coffee, he went to the front door and picked up the day's copy of The Crumb Herald.

But he was caught by the bold headline on the front page:

STAY INSIDE!

Looking further at the copy, he saw that every column of text was composed of the same two words, repeated over and over.

Stay inside! Stay inside! Stay inside! Stay inside! Stay inside! Stay inside!

He stood for a moment staring at the strange edition of the newspaper.

What's today's date? he thought. No, it's not Crumbfoolery Day.

While he puzzled over the strange paper, he closed the door and paced over to their telephone to call the editor of The Crumb Herald, Edgar Splind. He looked at the clock on the wall and knew it was early, but this seemed like a worthwhile reason to call.

He picked up the receiver and dialed Edgar's number. It rang four times before being answered by a groggy voice.

"Hello?" said Splind.

"Edward, it's Gurt. What is this in the paper?"

"What? What do you mean?" said the groggy voice, clearly still waking up.

"What do you mean by 'Stay inside,' exactly? Is it some sort of joke? You know Crumbfoolery Day isn't for three months."

"I don't know what you're talking about, Gurt. It's too early for this."

"Edgar, go look at your paper," demanded Gurt.

"Ok, hold on." The line was quiet for a minute as Gurt listened to Splind's feet treading away from the phone. Then, "Gurt, I don't know what this is…" His voice trailed off. He was audibly shaken.

Gurt heard him frantically flipping through the pages of the paper and muttering to himself. "Whaa…"

"Gurt, I'll have to call you back. I don't know what this is. I don't know who did this," said Splind, now fully awake.

"You didn't have anything to do with it?" asked Gurt.

"No, Gurt! We had a normal issue set to come out today. My daughter's recital details were going to be in it! I have to go," and the line went dead.

Officer Gurt hung up the telephone and looked back at the paper still in his hands. What a curious thing. Of course, it was far from the first curious thing to happen in Crumb Hill.

He flipped through the pages and each one said the same thing: Stay inside!

There must be something he was missing. He walked over to the stove, poured his coffee, and then sat at the table to more closely examine the paper. His wife had heard the conversation and come to the dining room too. Gurt showed her the paper and the two of them looked through it page by page.

His hunch was right: there was one small hint left on the inside of the last page. All of the headlines and columns said the same two words as all the rest, but there a clue as to what was going on. A little poem was printed at the very bottom of the page:

Dangling Jerry
smoking his chains
come out to play
and see what remains

2

Officer Gurt figured he'd better not go outside, since in Crumb Hill, when weird things happened or messages appeared, it was best to pay attention to them. But he was worried about the rest of the residents. Would they all stay inside? And what about those who didn't get the newspaper, or simply didn't look at it?

He looked again at the cryptic poem at the bottom of the last page. Everyone in Crumb Hill knew Dangling Jerry — the little beast who loved to hang from chains and chain smoke. Most of the time, that term means smoking a lot of cigarettes, but for Jerry it meant smoking his chains. He was addicted to them, so he'd smoke them while he hung from them.

But this was strange because there was no way he could pull off a stunt like changing all the copy in all of the newspapers in Crumb Hill. Either he had help, or someone was framing him, or at the very least, pointing to him.

Officer Gurt knew he had to get in contact with Jerry, which would be difficult because Jerry didn't have a telephone…or even a house. He just hung from his chains in random places around Crumb Hill.

Officer Gurt went upstairs to his bedroom window, which had a decent view over a good portion of Crumb Hill. He stood at the pane and scanned the yards, parks, and houses he could see. Several people were walking around as usual over in Crumb Park, and one couple was walking down his street, about to pass his house.

He yanked the window up and yelled down to them. "Hey, you two!"

The couple looked up and he saw that it was the Nattingers.

"Morning, Officer Gurt!" the man yelled back.

"Didn't you see the newspaper today??" he shouted, ignoring their greeting.

They stopped walking, intrigued. "No, officer. We stopped getting it years ago. It was nothing but So and so got thrown into The Dimension this week, and such and such monster crawled out of it this week."

Well now I know which radio stations they've been listening to, thought Officer Gurt to himself.

"So you didn't see the headlines today?" he yelled down to them.

"Well no, why?" shouted up Mr. Nattinger. "What did it say?"

"It just said 'Stay inside' over and over. I'm trying to figure out what it means and who wrote it."

"Oh, what does the article talk about?"

"Nothing. It's just those two words. Stay inside."

"Well that's curious. Can we look at it?"

"Sure."

He descended the stairs and met them at the front door, careful not to pass through the door frame, just in case. Even though the Nattingers were fine outside, Gurt wanted to be extra cautious. He opened the door and let them in. They walked to the dining room, where Mrs. Gurt sat with the paper on the table.

They greeted each other and the Nattingers looked at the paper for themselves, flipping through the pages and seeing that indeed, each page said the same two words.

"Well," said Mr. Nattinger, "clearly we were outside and nothing happened. It's some sort of hoax!" He chuckled to himself and they walked back to the front door.

"Well please be careful," said Mrs. Gurt warmly.

"We will and have a great day!" called back Mr. Nattinger over his shoulder. They stepped out the front door and Officer Gurt closed it behind them.

A moment later, the Gurts heard screams from outside. The screams lasted only a couple seconds and then stopped. Officer Gurt ran to the front door and looked through the peephole, but saw nothing. Just an empty street in front of their house.

He leapt up the stairs and ran to the window in their bedroom again. He looked down on the street before their house and still saw nothing. It appeared to be just a normal day. The Nattingers had vanished. There was no way they could have made it out of view that fast, yet they were nowhere to be seen.

He descended again to his wife with concern in his eyes. "They're gone."

"What happened?" she said, mainly to herself. "They were fine before they came in here…" her voice trailed off.

"Well I don't know, but I know two things: We are staying inside, and I need to find out how to get in touch with Dangling Jerry."

3

Officer Gurt's keen mind was piecing something together. The Nattingers didn't seem to be in any trouble outside until after they knew about the newspaper and its headlines. Perhaps people were only in danger when they read the paper. It gave him an idea for how to get in touch with Dangling Jerry.

He ran back up to his bedroom window, hoping more people would be walking by. No one was there, so he had to wait. He paced back and forth before the window for five minutes, then ten.

Finally, he saw someone walking down his street. As they got closer, he saw that it was two people: Martin and his Gleeb, Melk.

He opened the window, careful not to let any part of him go out through the frame.

"Martin!" he yelled down. "Hello, Melk!"

The pair looked up at him. "Good morning, officer!" yelled back Martin.

"Have you two seen Dangling Jerry today?" shouted back Officer Gurt.

"You know, we did see him chain smoking out in front of the old warehouse on Plum Street. He really got those chains heated up hot!"

"Well could I ask you two a favor then?" Officer Gurt didn't even pause for a reply. "Could I ask you to go up and tell him to come see me here at my home?"

Martin looked at Melk, puzzled by the request. Why couldn't Officer Gurt just go see Jerry himself?

Thinking quickly, Officer Gurt added, "My wife is sick and I can't just leave her alone, but I really need to speak to Jerry as soon as possible."

"Okay, if you really need him, I suppose…can we tell him what it's for?"

"The pape — " Gurt caught himself before it was too late. "The paper chains are better for smoking than the metal chains. I need to talk to him about…his health. But it's urgent."

Martin still looked confused, but he and Melk shuffled back the way they had come from, and Officer Gurt waited eagerly for Jerry to arrive.

Almost an hour later, there was a knock on the door. Officer Gurt rushed to it and swung it open. Just as he expected, there stood Martin, Melk and Dangling Jerry.

Jerry marched right in past Gurt and as he did, said, "Eyyy, you got shome plashes I could hang-gup theshe chains — eh?"

"I'm sorry Jerry," answered Gurt, "I don't think we have any dangling spots in here, but I won't keep you long." He turned to Martin and Melk and said, "Thank you both for bringing him. I hope you enjoy the rest of your day!" and shut the door. He felt bad being so curt to the pair, but he also knew it was for their own good.

From the dining room, he heard "What'sh thish?" and knew Jerry had found the paper.

He walked over and explained everything to Danging Jerry. He told him about how there was supposed to be a normal paper, but no one knows why it sent this. Then he told him about the Nattingers, and how they disappeared when they went back outside.

"Shoundsh like The Dimension to me," said Jerry. "Alsho, didn't you now make it sho I can't go outshide now?"

"Well yes, I suppose that's the case," said Officer Gurt. "I'm sorry, I guess you'll need to stay here with us until this is resolved."

"Well then I'll need a plashe to hang up my chainsh and dangle for a bit."

Officer Gurt looked at his wife and shrugged. He hadn't thought this all the way through. But then he realized he'd left out the most important part. He flipped to the back page and showed Jerry the poem.

"I almost forgot! This is why I invited you here. It seems to be pointing directly at you! Do you know anything about this?"

Jerry looked at the poem and then started laughing. "Well firsht of all, I can't read. But if it says what you shaid it shays, then I know exactly who you need to talk to next."

"And who would that be?" interjected Mrs. Gurt, now curious herself.

"Well, Principal Bearhair of courshe!"

"You mean… the glops and goops of him that came back from the black cube? From The Dimension?" asked Officer Gurt.

"Well yesh!" Jerry looked at both of them and then explained more. "I dangle all over Crumb Hill, right? Right. Sho, I hear things and I shee thingsh. Shometimes, people shay things because they don't know I'm nearby, dangling. But I lishten. In fact, I tried to get shome of my friends to call me The Lishtener. The Lishtener of Crumb Hill. Got a nice shound to it, eh?"

Officer Gurt racked his brain to figure out who Dangling Jerry's friends could be, but continued listening.

"Sho, a few nights ago, I hear what's left of Principal Bearhair gooping hish way down the block. I hear whishpers. He's talking to shomeone, but I can't shee who. I hear the other guy shay shomething about The Dimension and shome monshters or shomething. I lishtened real good, and I hear them shake shlimy hands and make a deal."

"Did you hear what the deal was?" asked Gurt.

He looked straight at Officer Gurt.

"Yesh, but I needsh to dangle now."

4

They found a place in the basement where Jerry could dangle. They set up some bolts in the rafters and hooked him up so he could have a nice long hang. But the Gurts were clear that he is not to smoke his chains in the house.

After Jerry had dangled for a while, Officer Gurt went to ask him more questions. He descended the stairs and Jerry was hanging there, gently swaying back and forth from his chains which made a faint metallic creaking sound.

"So what was the deal Principal Hairbear made?" he asked the creature.

"Well, he wantsh to get hish body back, right? He doeshn't want to be a pile of shloppy goop for the resht of his life, right?"

Officer Gurt nodded along.

"Sho, the deal was, he'd get his body back to the way it wash before he had a little munch from The Dimension beast. And in exchange, he would open the hatch that letsh the beasts in."

"What hatch?" Officer Gurt was confused. "Everyone knows that no one can choose to come back from The Dimension. There are only entrances to it, not exits. Bearhair got lucky when it spat him and Timmy back out!"

Dangling Jerry looked straight at Officer Gurt. "You don't know about the hatch?"

"Where is it? What is it?" Gurt was getting worked up.

"It's out in the woodsh on the path to the Tonic Woman'sh place. I have a little poem to remember where it is:

"In the trunk of a tree,
you move a few leaves,
and you tug on the root
and you unleash the beasht."

Gurt paused, waiting for more. "That's it?"

"That'sh it."

"That doesn't tell me anything about where it is. There are a million trees on the path to the Tonic Woman's."

"Well yesh. But I know what tree it is."

"So it doesn't help me at all??" Gurt yelled at the dangling creature.

"Well I'll go with you to look at it. But we can't go now becaushe we can't go outshide."

"Oh…right." Gurt thought over what he'd just heard. "So, Hairbear would open this hatch in the tree to let some beasts in from The Dimension, and in exchange, he would get his body back so he's not a sludgy mess?"

"Think sho."

"And you don't know who he made this deal with?"

"Right."

"So there are monsters from The Dimension running around and taking people when they go outside right now. But then how did that get in the newspaper, and how would it know when people read their paper or not? And why would they frame you?"

Jerry thought about this for a moment while hanging from his chains.

"Maybe they know I heard them. They could have heard my chainsh and knew I had information. I don't know, Offisher."

Things began to come together in Officer Gurt's mind. He went back upstairs to call Splind again.

"Ok, Splind, you need to be honest with me this time. What was your deal with Bearhair?"

"I'm sorry, Officer, I don't know what you mean."

"You made a deal with him to open the hatch and let the beasts in. Why would you want them running all over Crumb Hill and taking our people??"

The line was silent for a moment. Gurt thought the line had gone dead. Suddenly he heard Splind crying. "I'm sorry, officer!" he sobbed some more. "My little daughter — sob — she fell into the entrance to The Dimension in the woods, behind the Old Crumb Factory." He sniffled.

"Okay," said Officer Gurt. "So then what did you do?"

"Well I went back looking for her and saw that an entrance to The Dimension had opened up. And you know the saying, 'If you yell into the abyss, the abyss will yell back to you.' So I did, and a voice called back to me. It said that if I open the hatch, it'll spit my daughter back out."

"So that's why you let all the monsters out?"

"No. I was conflicted. I would never just let monsters from The Dimension run amuck in our town."

"But then Principal Hairbear sweetened the deal?"

Splind's voice was still shaky. "H-he wants his body back, and apparently The Dimension had talked to him too."

"What were you going to get from him?"

"He was going to subscribe to the newspaper."

Officer Gurt was shocked. He expected a massive exchange of money, or a wild favor.

"That's it? Just subscribe to the paper?"

"Yes, our readership is down." When Officer Gurt didn't reply, he went on. "We are down to eight houses. You are one of eight people to get it still. So now we have nine with the Bearhairs."

"I can't believe this," muttered Gurt.

"I'm sorry officer," Splid said, crying again. "I wanted to save my daughter and my paper. I didn't want anyone to get hurt, which is why I tried to warn everyone to stay inside today!"

"Well I have one more question. Why would people only get taken by the monsters when they knew about the paper? What difference did that make?"

Splind thought about this for a moment. "I have a theory. Haven't you heard that the beasts can smell fear?"

"Yes, everyone in Crumb Hill knows that."

"So maybe it's just those who were warned, they become afraid and then become targets for the monsters."

"So basically," said Gurt, restraining his anger, "you simply made targets out of everyone who gets your newspaper by making them afraid?"

Splind was silent again. "Well…when you put it like that…"

"Now we just need to figure out how to shut the hatch and get the beasts back to The Dimension."

"I might have an idea," said Splind.

And Gurt hoped he was right, because so far, Splind had just made this whole day a disaster.

5

"My plan will work if we can get in touch with the Tonic Woman," said Splind through the phone line. "She always knows how to open and close The Dimension and work her magic."

"But her tricks don't always work," said Officer Gurt. "They worked with Timmy and Bearhair, but they don't always."

"Well, I mean, Bearhair is a moving pile of sloppy guts and Timmy is two-dimensional… And we don't know what happened to Little Bailee."

"True. So what is your plan?"

"Well like I said, we need to get in touch with the Tonic Woman."

"I can talksh to her," said a voice behind Gurt. He turned and saw that the little creature named Dangling Jerry had come up the stairs and overheard his conversation.

"You can?" asked Gurt. "How?"

"Eashy. She gave me her number," replied Jerry.

"No she didn't, she doesn't have a telephone!"

"Yesh she doesh, she's just particular in who she gives her number to," said Jerry coolly.

Gurt was baffled. Why would the Tonic Woman of Crumb Hill give this little beast her number? He got off the line with Splind and let Jerry dial the number (Jerry made him turn around as he did).

Gurt listened as Jerry began talking to the mysterious woman.

"Mmmhmm….Yesh. No, jusht today…. Yesh. No, but I can ashk." Jerry turned away from the phone and asked Gurt, "Do you have any dynamite?"

Gurt was shocked, then answered, "Uh, maybe at the station?"

"Maybe at the station," Jerry said into the phone. "Mmmhmm. Yesh. Mmmhmm. Ok, thank you. Bye," and he hung up.

"Well, we need the dynamite," said Jerry. "And, she said, the entrances and exits to The Dimension have different rulesh every day. And only she knowsh what they are."

"So did she say what we need to do today?" asked Gurt.

"Yesh, here ish the plan. It all hash to be done by 1:17, sho we only have one chance…" and the creature explained it all to him.

-

An hour later, Gurt had called one of his deputies to bring him as much dynamite as he could.

"That's an awful lot of 'splosive," he said.

"Yup," said Gurt. "We have to be sure it works the first time. We have one shot."

Gurt then told him what to do. He and Jerry told the deputy which tree to set all the explosives on, and to blow them at exactly 1:17. He did not tell him about the hatch or the beasts or the newspaper.

"Uh, you're sure about this Officer?" asked the young deputy.

"Nope. But it's the best shot we have." Then he added, "and if you see Principal Hairbear sliming his way around town, feel free to invite him to come watch the explosion with you. It may be good to give him something to do."

-

Half an hour later, things were in place. At least, Gurt thought so. He assumed the deputy would have the dynamite wired about now, and he hoped Bearhair would be near.

And all he and Jerry had to do was step outside his home right at 1:17. Currently it was 1:15 and he kept nervously checking his watch. He and Jerry and his wife stood inside the front door.

They had one shot.

The Tonic Woman had said that the beasts would come running for them as soon as they stepped outside. Then the dynamite would blow up the hatch and for just a moment, there would be a tear in The Dimension that would suck in the monsters and squirt out Splind's daughter.

1:16.

Gurt had his hand on the doorknob and could feel his heart pounding out of his shirt.

Ten seconds.

Then he was turning the knob and they were stepping outside. He heard the furious patter of footsteps rushing toward them, standing on his porch. The beasts were moving too fast to be seen. He braced for the impact, preparing to be dragged to The Dimension. His eyes were closed tight.

Then he heard what sounded like a strong wind, or some sort of gigantic suction. The sound of the beasts was gone.

Then a moment later, he heard the delayed boom. The deputy had done it!

Gurt took another step out onto the porch, then onto the street.

Nothing happened.

The Tonic Woman's crazy plan had worked.

But suddenly he heard a scream coming from high above him. He looked up and saw a large, round girl falling down toward the street. The scream got louder as she hurtled closer.

-

She hit the street twenty feet from Gurt and again, he flinched as she struck the pavement, hard.

But then she bounced up, dozens of feet into the air. She kept screaming.

She came down in his neighbor's back yard and launched up again ten feet into the air. This hopped her over the fence and into the Gurts' back yard.

They ran through the house and found her lying there, unable to get up because of her rotund middle.

"Splind?" asked Mrs. Gurt. "Are you Splind's daughter?"

"Yah," she replied from the far side of her bulbous body.

As they got closer, they realized her skin was made of tough rubber and she seemed to be filled with air. She was crying — shocked and confused.

"Wh-where am I?" she asked.

"You're back in Crumb Hill," answered Mrs. Gurt gently.

"I-I was in this place where everything was balloons. I was bouncing around on them. There were so many colors." She cried a bit more. "And then I bounced too high and it felt like I got launched out of the atmosphere, then I landed back down here and bounced around."

Mrs. Gurt continued to comfort her until the deputy arrived to debrief Officer Gurt.

He also seemed to be in shock, but unharmed.

"Well, I did find Principal Bearhair…but…but I think he's gone."

"What happened?" asked Officer Gurt.

"Well, I had everything wired up and from behind me, I hear someone gooping around. I turn and sure enough, it was Principal Hairbear. He was looking all suspisious. I mean, I know he's just a pile of guts, but he was acting suspicious.

"It was pretty simple. I waited till 1:17, and pulled the detonator. It exploded. But then…then I see all these beasts flying past me, faster than a horse, and they're going right into the hole I just made with the explosion.

"Then I hear screaming and look and bit by bit, Principal Hairbear is being sucked into the hole too. But weirdest thing, I don't feel it sucking me in at all. I just stood there. Then after all of Hairbear was sucked in, I hear this escalating sound of a loud wind. Then a pop and kind of, excuse me officer, kind of like a fart? Like breaking wind? And it shoots a little girl out of the hole, high into the sky."

Officer Gurt pointed out the back window to where Mrs. Gurt was still talking to Little Splind.

"Yes! Her! She shot out of the hole! And then finally everything was quiet and then I came here."

"Well good work, deputy," said Gurt. "We pulled that off perfectly."

The deputy looked confused. "You're not going to tell me what happened?"

"Maybe someday. Well, to be honest, I'm not entirely sure myself how it all works here. Just know for now that you did it perfectly, saved some people from The Dimension, and sometimes…that's just the way things go here in Crumb Hill."

the end

Dangling Jerry when he was just in his larval stage.

Advertisement

Don't do your shovel work without...

"SROOF FFOFFOO'S"

*Not recommended by any doctors, engineers, dentists, or the Tonic Woman.

The children of Crumb Hill Elementary got to play with some visitors from The Dimension today! Although we do not condone science, we love our guests! The visitors said they would love to come back as long as we keep throwing our cats into The Dimension!

Smoking is cool if you're Gleeb. NOT if you're human! They need it to cleanse their gills. In humans, smoke just hurts our organs.

"Every night before bed, they tell me a story. Sometimes it's about the Crumb Wars, sometimes The Dimension, and sometimes it's about a dog who didn't like his tail so he rubbed it off on a tree."

22 pieces of wisdom

from my 22 years

by the Tonic Woman

The Tonic Woman of Crumb Hill sat down with us to share some life wisdom.

On my 22nd birthday, I want to share some of my findings; things life has taught me in my brief stint in Crumb Hill so far!

1. If you yell long into The Dimension, The Dimension will yell back into you.

2. Do not pet a burning beast.

3. Yes, I'm really 22. Why do you keep asking me that? What…do I not look it?

4. Most healing tonics only require four mice and a little smile.

5. No, I don't have a birth certificate. I don't even think Crumb Hospital issues those. Do you always ask interviewees for their birth certificate?

6. Smoking chains can cause short-term memory loss. It can also cause short-term memory loss.

7. The ads were true: You can actually save 15% or more on Dimension Insurance with the Crumb Hill Gecko. Anyone who is remotely financially responsible would switch over. (He didn't pay me to say that, it's just plain smart!)

8. If you go to bed later and wake up earlier, you'll have more day to use.

9. Yes, twenty-two. Two, two. Why do you keep asking me about this? Wait, these count as my bits of wisdom??

10. Try to care less what others think about you.

11. Don't make a fuss about whether someone calls it Kristerkin or Crumbmas; it's the same holiday and we need to be united, not divided!

12. Don't spend it all in one place! (your life) (unless that place is Crumb Hill, then that's okay.

13. Yes! Oh my Drog. I was born 22 years ago, today. It's my birthday. If you ask me about my age again, I'm gonna go mix up a tonic behind my house and you won't like it.

14. What?

15. Oh, I said I'll mix up a tonic behind my house and you won't like it.

16. What was that?

17. Yah, a tonic. It will give you a tail. That's the one I was thinking to do to you. Do you want a tail?

18. Yes, a tail from your lower back. Where else would it be?

19. I don't know, I imagine you'd still be able to poop. Animals have tails and can still poop.

20. Wait, you *want* a tail now? As long as you can still poop?

21. How many pieces of wisdom do I have left?

22. Okay, okay, contrary to popular sentiment, animal bones hung around your home do not protect you from beasts from The Dimension.

23. Don't look at the crumb in your brother's eye when you have a hill in your own.

24. Yes, I know I've gone over 22 pieces of wisdom now. I'm going to make a tonic.

25. Yes, fine. I'll give you the tail tonic. Just leave me alone.

26. Yes, I'm really 22.

PUBLIC SERVICE ANNOUNCEMENT!

We are annoyed that we must ask you again to please stop playing with the scarecrows. Your friends won't think you're cool.

Just stop.

Advertisement

Here's a sneak preview of Crumb Hill's newest talkie

"Never Go To Sleep, Never Whisper, Everyone is Happy"

"Yom youm yom.
churdlen eN my tommy.
  Num noum nuUm.
Churdlen taste betTer en Crumm."

-a poem by BEest

Various Crumb Hill neighborhoods lining up for their daily Rations at 1:17. Residents know not to fight for a place in line, or hassle the deliverer. That's why they say, "If you stir up some action, you don't get your Ration!"

Crumb Hill Prison

an unflinching look at the dampest prison in the world

"Just look at the reviews!" boasted Warden Knut. He wagged a recent edition of *The Crumb Herald* in our face and we certainly saw the reviews, right there on the front page. The headline read, "Crumb Hill Prison has been voted 'Dampest prison in the country'!!"

"It's so damp it's nearly wet!" said one inmate.

"Yes it is very damp. I don't get why they're proud of that," stated another.

We had seen enough. We asked the warden to show us around and tell us all about the facility and its programs.

"Oh, with pleasure!" he replied, beaming. "It is so very damp."

We first went to the wash rooms, where the prisoners are bathed with tear-free shampoo so their eyes don't hurt. They are, however, scrubbed down with metal wire brushes which scrape off their scabs, which, ironically, they received from the wire brushes last time they were bathed.

"Can't have 'em scabbed up," said Warden Knut, "but we really want their eyes to be ok. They can be so sensitive. So many shampoos just sting so dang much."

Next, we were led outside to the yard where some of the voluntary inmates were practicing their tap dance routine. We did not have a chance to speak to them, because their music was blasting so loud and their rhythmic claps drowned out our words. They seemed to have been having a good time though, so after watching their dance routine a few times through, we

Above: Voluntary inmates hanging out by their cells. You can tell they have smoked a lot of chains. **Below:** Tap dance lessons in the yard.

moved on to another cell block.

It was here I got to speak directly to one of the voluntary inmates, and the warden even gave us a few minutes of privacy while he ran to go put out a fire. Apparently some Gleeb had figured out how to use a magnifying glass.

I sat down with Danny Quick, who told me about what life is really like in the dampest prison in the country.

"It's really not too bad," he began, sitting on the corner of his mattress. "The warden is pretty good to us, but they really can be pretty rough with the wire brushes."

Quick explained that the tearless shampoo really was a big draw for him, and the dance sessions in the yard are great exercise. "My calves have never burned like they did after my first tap session!"

When asked if there are any downsides to life in Crumb Hill Prison, Danny Quick was quick to respond.

"Oh yes. You see these guys behind me? Don't look at them. Don't use your eyes, use your periphery. You see them?"

I did, and a chill ran down my spine by simply becoming aware of their presence. I hadn't noticed these floating beings hovering just beyond Danny, in the room with us. They looked like sheets from the bed had risen up and looked over to the conversation. We asked Quick what they were.

"Oh, I don't know what they are, like, ontologically, but I just refer to them as The Singers. They like to sing my cellmates and I to sleep…but sometimes their singing actually keeps me awake."

We asked Danny what they sing about.

"Oh all sorts of things. Crumb Hill, moisture, sleep, friendship, ceramics. Their favorite seems to be this one they sing every other night. It goes like this — "

Then he sang in a higher-pitched, soft and gentle voice:

> *Softly, very very softly,*
> *listen to the water drip.*
> *Gently, always walking gently,*
> *careful that you do not slip.*

Slowly, we will lay you slowly,
down into an endless sleep.
Deeply, very very deeply,
your rest will be so very deep.

Body, we don't have a body,
but we can always find a way.
Ever, sweetly and forever,
asleep you will forever stay.

He finished singing his tune, paused, and then exclaimed, "Man! It always gives me the creeps. Why would they want anyone to stay asleep forever? Makes me scared I won't ever wake up. So that's why sometimes I can't fall asleep."

He paused again.

"Yah, I guess that's really the only downside of living here though. The rest of it is pretty nice."

As if on a timer, Warden Knut returned just then and we wrapped up our tour.

As we walked toward the exit through another cell block, the warden explained that they have been having a lot of trouble with chain smoking. "There are always a lot of guys smuggling chains in here and we can't seem to disrupt the flow."

We asked if there are a lot of fights or other problems in the prison, as there are in prisons in other parts of the world.

"Not really, honestly," he replied. "Since they're voluntary inmates, we don't see too much of that in here. Sometimes you get personalities that just don't mesh well. Sometimes there are philosophical or political disagreements. One guy is big on The Dimension, and another is a Dimension denier; one guy voted for Mayor Tuggs, another wanted Pippington to get elected, you know?"

When we asked what happens when these disagreements arise, he said, "Oh they may be pushing and shoving. Sometimes they'll start throwing haymakers and we need to separate them. There have only been a few times we've had to transport someone out of the prison and toss them in The Dimension—"

He suddenly stopped, realizing that he had overstepped. In Crumb Hill, capital punishment is not allowed, and voluntary prisoners are never to be thrown into The Dimension.

"That wasn't on the record, right?" he said with a chuckle. "You know I was just kidding, right? We would never throw an inmate into The Dimension!" He began sweating profusely. "You're not going to publish that, right?" he asked.

We told him we weren't sure. The problem for Warden Knut was, he had said that in a cell block with plenty of voluntary inmates well within earshot. As we walked out of the hallway, there was a big red button by the door.

We made sure our crew left first, then I turned and bid adieu to Warden Knut. I pushed the big red button which opened all the cell doors, then slammed the door shut quickly, with the warden still trapped in the hallway with many of his inmates.

The Crumb Hill Aquatic Deep Sea Department (CHADS-D) has been scouring our waters for the Lost Letter, rumored to have the secret of our town's origins.

"It's either in here or it got dropped into The Dimension, or I left it in my sock drawer," said the lead searcher.

Little Billy Puddles was born with a strange gift. Every time he laughs, someone gets thrust back from The Dimension...which usually causes more harm than good. So he tries not to laugh!

The Building

a story from the city outside of Crumb Hill

The building went up faster than any before it ever had. The permits sliced through the red tape of the city like a knife through butter. Zoning and construction permits passed effortlessly through the various hands of bureaucratic offices that normally hold up construction for months, yet the ground was broken on this building within days.

Initially, no one realized what an amazing feat this was. To the outside eyes like mine, it seemed like nothing more than another skyscraper being put up in a city riddled with them.

It wasn't until a few weeks into the build that word began to get out about the mysterious new addition to the city, and the one behind the project. The news registers named the man behind the project as one Mr. Nephilous Krimm. Once the news broke the stories about the man and his skyscraper, people became even more curious both about him and his building. Yet, despite the headlines, everyone I talked to was unable to find anything about him at all. He seemed to not exist, according to city records and newspapers and hospital birth certificates. I had one friend who contacted nearly every hospital in the state to find information about the man. But he came up empty.

Most people had no idea what he looked like either. Unlike other wealthy businessmen, Mr. Krimm was not featured posing with a shovel at the groundbreaking, or in front of the construction machines as the work began. One construction worker I talked to claims to have seen his leg and shoe as he turned around a corner near the construction site, but didn't see his face.

He famously refused interviews, though his responses were polite and intriguing. To one newspaper he wrote,

"Thank you for thinking of me and my project, but I am inextricably bound to my work and unable to peel myself away from this very important work. Please feel free to write about the tower as it rises, but I am unable to provide further comment on the situation. I wish you all the best. NK"

The paper ran his response and of course the town went wild, and his ominous language only made us all more intrigued.

For the next few months, the tower went up with just as little information being released. After the first couple floors were completed, however, something became glaringly obvious that set this building apart from every other skyscraper in the city, if not the world: There were no windows. It was a solid wall. It was beige and seemed unfinished or hasty, like an adobe texture. It did not seem like the sort of exterior for a skyscraper created by a mysterious, wealthy hermit.

The tower rose higher and higher as the months went on. It began to look like a ragged finger rising up in the midst of the city, pointing at the sky. If it was a finger, it looked like it was accusing the sky of something, or perhaps rising in a triumphal victory gesture.

By winter it was dozens of stories high, approaching the heights of some of the highest buildings in the city. It still looked crazy, without a single window visible.

One day I tried to get close and ask one of the workers some questions. I paced the sidewalk leading up to the odd building and tried to catch someone dressed like a worker going in or coming out. But there was no one. Attempting not to look conspicuous, I paced around the block a few times. Eventually a full hour passed and I hadn't seen anyone come in or go out of the spot that looked like the front door. I decided to walk right up to it and look through the window.

I crossed the street and turned on the sidewalk toward it. Right as I got close to the glass door, someone came out of it. It was a short, middle-aged woman. She marched right up to me and, not very politely, asked if she could help me.

I was stunned. I hadn't prepared to explain why I was snooping around the building. She could clearly see my confusion and reached up to touch my forearm.

"Perhaps it's better if you walk away and come back another day." She offered me a joyless smile and abruptly turned and walked back into the doors. From where I stood, the doors appeared to be glass, yet I couldn't see a single thing on the other side of them. They were highly reflective and perhaps it was dark on the inside? It was impossible to see anything inside, but I dared not get closer to them and try to peer in.

And now, back to your story!

2

More months passed and everyone agreed that the building had shot up far faster than any other before it. Were they bypassing building and safety codes? All we could do was speculate. When the newspaper ran a story about it, it told us what we already knew (that the building was going up fast) mixed with some pundit's speculation about it. Krimm hadn't made any statements since the first one.

The building seemed to be nearing completion, as the rough, windowless adobe-looking material looked like it would curve to a domed close at the top. It truly looked like a pale finger pointing at the heavens. All that was left was the very tip of the finger. It looked like the construction was a mere week away from closing the finger and dubbing the building completed.

I kept a closer eye on the building the next few days. That Tuesday on my morning commute, it looked like the top of the finger had come together. On my evening commute, I saw a crowd gathering at the base of the building, right at the door where I had tried to look in months earlier.

Of course, I couldn't help myself and approached the outside of the crowd. People were muttering about Nephilous Krimm making a speech to mark the completion of his tower. It couldn't have been more than 20 minutes before the crowd fell silent and a figure came out through the glass door.

He stood on a small podium and raised a hand, both to greet and quiet us. He looked just like any other business man, with a suit and tie. His hair looked flawlessly combed and neat. He stood confident and tall. He smiled deep into his cheeks and seemed like he could win over any person standing in this crowd.

"Hello everyone," he began. The city street was utterly silent. A baby cried two blocks away.

"Thank you for coming to the grand opening of my building. It will be some magnificent work we will accomplish here. If anyone would like to work with me, simply quit your job and be here tomorrow morning at 8am and we will begin. Thank you." He waved again to the crowd and turned and walked back through the front door.

The crowd remained silent for a full minute, wanting there to be more. More information, more details. Perhaps even more of the intriguing presence of Mr. Krimm himself. Once the chatter of the crowd started again, I overheard numerous people near me say that they were going to inform their boss that they quit, and they'd show up here tomorrow at 8am. Krimm had that sort of sway over people, to engage them and win them over to himself.

I walked home. As much as my curiosity wanted to drop everything and show up tomorrow morning, I couldn't justify leaving everything behind just for one man I'd heard speak once.

The following days, I heard about the swarms of men who showed up that morning to work for the mysterious Nephilous Krimm. I saw photos in the paper of the hundreds of men gathered outside the front door of the windowless building. The report said that not a single person was turned away for a job. Every single one was welcomed in. The paper did mention, however, that they were unable to attain a comment from anyone who had gone to work for him. It was as if they went in but didn't come out.

As I passed by the building on my daily commute, I always glanced over toward the building and saw small crowds of people. Some were simply observing, others were trying to get in to work for Krimm.

Over the following weeks, the hubbub died down around the building, as there were no new updates. The tall, pale finger of the skyscraper sat there, looking dead except for the small crowd always congregated at its base. Nephilous Krimm was silent and the newspapers couldn't come up with anything noteworthy to say about it that hadn't been said before.

Then one Thursday, the men appeared in the streets. There were hundreds of them wearing strange uniforms, unlike anything I'd seen before.

Compilation of photos of the men.

They seemed to endlessly stream out from Krimm's building and spread throughout the entire city. They walked with intention, splitting off in groups to walk to every part of the city. Within a few hours that Thursday, they were posted everywhere in the city. You couldn't walk more than two blocks without seeing at least one group of them, monitoring and patrolling the streets.

They didn't do anything, however. They didn't say anything or interact with anyone on the streets. They didn't seem particularly interested in enforcing anything. In fact, if it weren't for their uniforms and masks, they would have looked just like any normal person going for a stroll through the city streets. Initially there was a lot of confusion and intrigue over these groups of uniformed men walking the streets in their strange outfits, but they didn't bother anyone. And of course, there is no law against wearing matching clothes in big groups and wandering the streets of our city.

The newspapers were abuzz with speculation and theories about the men. None of them would answer any questions from reporters or civilians. They didn't even seem to speak to one another, but it was hard to tell because of the masks they wore. So all that was left for us was more speculation.

By Saturday we had nearly gotten used to the guards' presence posted all over the city. They didn't bother anyone, or really do much of anything.

But on Sunday, everything changed.

3

…But on Sunday, everything changed.

I happened to be walking through the town, just a few blocks from the Krimm building. Suddenly, there was a deafening crack that ripped through the air. It was as loud as a bomb, but sounded like rocks being torn apart. I looked toward the building–the location of the sound–and saw that it was falling apart!

Thousands of cracks ran down the sides of the building and chunks were falling off of it, crashing to the ground. It was like the hatching of an egg, with the outer shell of the building explosively falling apart. But when each piece hit the ground, it was surrounded by a cloud of dust and essentially vaporized. It was as if the outer shell of the building were made of mere dust that was barely held together. As the outer wall of the building fell apart, it seemed to cause little, if any damage when it struck the ground. Bits even fell on cars and people, but there was no damage from where I could see. They all seemed fine.

I had become distracted watching the pieces of the shell fall to the ground, throwing up massive clouds of dust, that I didn't notice what was being revealed. There was another building nested inside the shell. It appeared somewhat normal, except that instead of windows, there were what appeared to be massive eyeballs. There were hundreds of them. It was as if

someone took an ordinary skyscraper and replaced every window with an eyeball. They were moving constantly, glancing all over the city, watching everything.

From the central and tall vantage point, it felt like the eyes could see everywhere in the city. The eyes could see almost everywhere, and they were scanning every block, every street, every person. It felt like they could see into every single room in the city. There were hundreds if not thousands of eyes, scanning all over the entire city. I was too stunned by this strange sight to move or look away.

Suddenly I felt a hand grab my arm. I jerked my head away from the building to realize it was one of Krimm's minions grabbing me.

Before I could speak or ask why he was grabbing me, he firmly pulled my arm to walk with him and said, "Let's keep moving. No need to look at Mr. Krimm."

He had a firm grip on my arm for nearly a full block, walking me along briskly until I was more removed from the tower. I could still see it over the top of some buildings, but didn't have a direct view of it. I felt the eyes on me. The minion said nothing else, he just released my arm with a little shove and returned to his post.

I had no idea what to think and wandered home in a daze.

For the next few days, I was too nervous to leave my house for fear that the eyes would see me again and assume I was doing something wrong. I didn't want to feel another firm grip on my arm and be moved along, or worse, 'arrested,' as I had seen many people be lately. People were confused by this, because as far as we knew, Krimm was not the law. He was not associated with the government, yet he was arresting people as if he had the authority.

I heard one story from a neighbor that the police had resisted Krimm's minions, and from his tower he saw this, and sent more of his minions as reinforcements until there were so many of them they overwhelmed the police. All the officers were bound with some strange type of rope and taken into the tower. We don't know what happened to them after that.

We didn't hear of any other instances of the police pushing back against Krimm. Perhaps they simply acknowledged that he had bested them, that his forces were stronger than theirs. He had the advantage of surveillance; he could instantly see everything happening in the city and direct his men to wherever they needed to go in an instant. The police had nothing close to this, just their walkie talkies.

Krimm's eyes had won him the city.

Over the following months, more and more people gave in to the power of the building. It was futile to push back against him. You couldn't get within a mile of the tower without its countless eyes seeing you, and sending men to come stop you.

Fewer people walked on the streets. I heard rumors about tunnels being utilized by citizens to get around more effectively. This lasted a few weeks until Krimm's men began patrolling them as well. And a little while after that, eyes were installed along all the tunnels as well. Rather than cables or wires connecting them, they seemed to be connected to the tower with the same organic-looking rope that the police had been bound with. It was like a giant vein or organ. The red rope ran along the top of the tunnels, and all tunnels eventually made their way back to the tower.

Even under the earth, Krimm could see everything.

It seemed that this is how life would be from now on, until I had an idea.

Advertisement

THIS PUBLICATION IS BROUGHT TO YOU BY...

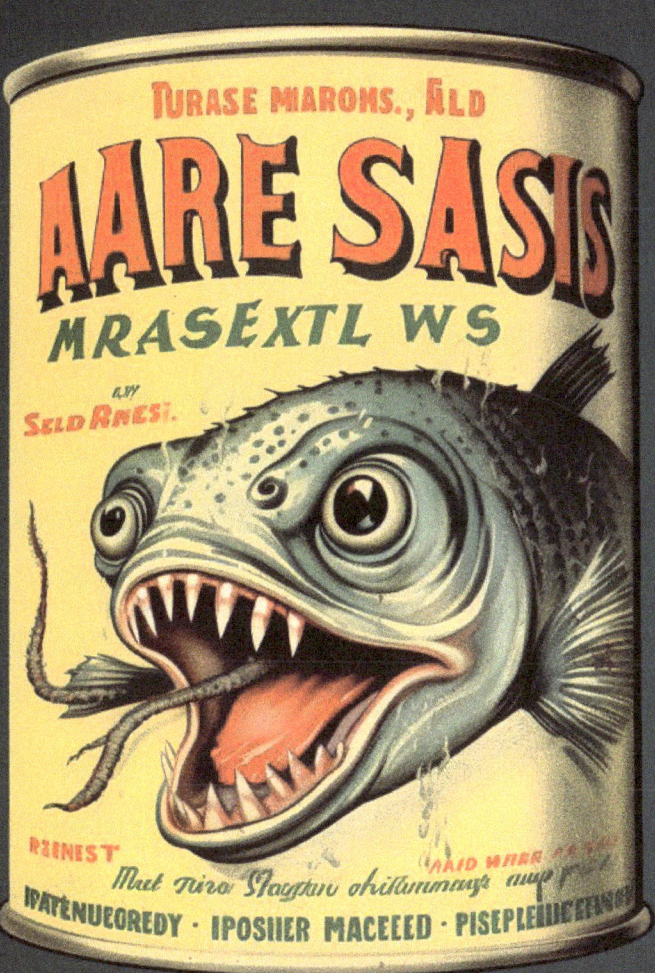

"STOP CALLING IT FISH!"

*Only take if you are pregnant, or want to be.

And now, back to your story!

4

It seemed that Krimm had no blindness. That was his aim after all: to see everything in the city, at once, not missing a thing.

Living under a new regime that had arisen with next to no resistance meant that this was all anyone talked or thought about. We could not talk about it in public, because although it was obvious that Krimm saw everything, it was assumed that he also heard everything, though we had no direct evidence of this.

I thought about this day and night. What's the one thing that someone who has eyes everywhere can't see? What's the one thing that he whose ears litter the streets can't hear? It plagued the back of my mind like an ongoing riddle.

It seemed like Krimm had thought of everything. We daily heard stories of attempted resistance and subsequent arrests. It even felt like his eyes could somehow see through walls and roofs. There was no escape from his all-seeing eyes; no place was safe from his gaze.

So one day, for no other reason than that my curiosity had grown to border violence, I stood on my front door step and stared at his building. The eyes were in constant motion, as always. A thousand eyes scanned every iota of the city, in constant motion. I stood there, gazing intently at the tower until, I couldn't be certain, but I swore that one of the eyes stopped moving and locked onto me.

I stared back.

It didn't move, but looked right at me standing in my doorway.

It wasn't more than sixty seconds until I saw two guards turn the corner onto my block, walking right toward me. I took a step back into my door when one of them called out.

"Citizen. Mr. Krimm wants to know why you were staring at his tower."

I took another step back into my home and was about to close the door when one of their gloved hands slapped against the door and pushed it open. He matched my steps — as I stepped backwards, he proceeded into my home. The other one stood in the doorway and stopped.

"Can I help you?" I asked the guard while still retreating back into my home.

He repeated himself. "Mr. Krimm would like to know why you were staring at him."

I didn't know how to answer, or what sort of response would best satisfy them. I kept backing up.

5

The guard was several inches taller than me, so I felt like a child as he advanced further into my home, right where I wanted to draw him into. I backed into my kitchen and pulled the lever I had rigged. It pulled a string through several hooks that led it up and along the ceiling to the front door. It released a sledgehammer that had been fixed up above the door, and now swung down and into the face of the guard at the door. It

swung in a perfect arc, and my estimation of his height and placement had been perfect. It appeared to hit him right in the nose beneath his mask, and he crumpled to the ground right in the doorway.

This all happened so fast that the minion who was now in my kitchen wasn't even aware that his partner was down before I grabbed the pot of boiling oil I had left on the stove and threw it on his face. Even through his mask, it burned his skin. It hit some exposed parts of his neck and ran down his torso.

He screamed and fell to the ground as well, clawing the mask from his head and wiping at his face. The skin was burned and melting. He kept crying out and I grew worried one of my neighbors — or worse, Krimm — would hear.

While he cried out, I quickly ran to my doorway and pulled the other guard inside, slamming the door closed and praying that the eyes hadn't seen what I just did. They could clearly see my doorway from the tower, but there was a small sliver of hope that none of them had been watching during those few seconds.

Now there were two men in my home: One unconscious and one screaming in agony from his burning skin. I figured it would only be a matter of time before he went into shock from the pain, but I figured I could help him along. I had a bottle of ether on my counter, which I now poured onto the rag by the sink and held it over his mouth, telling myself it was the most merciful thing I could do. The man whose skin was still bubbling fell silent and breathed in small, shallow breaths on my kitchen floor.

I returned to the man by the front door and began removing his uniform. I now realized that to put them on, both would be too large for me, and I had to choose between a mask filled with blood or a mask filled with oil and burnt skin. I opted for the bloody mask after a thorough scrubbing. I knew I had to work quickly before the men woke up, so I put on the uniform, rolled up the pant legs and tucked them into the boots so they didn't look so long, and scrubbed the inside of the mask with bleach.

But then I realized my miscalculation: the minions never traveled alone. There were always at least two or three walking together. Would Nephilous Krimm see this from his tower and be suspicious about the lone minion?

I decided to tie up the one who now lay in his underwear, so that when he woke up, he wouldn't be able to get out. Once he was secured, still bleeding profusely from his nose and mouth, I returned to the guard in my kitchen. I pulled his mask back over his face and dragged him to the front door by the wrists.

I opened the front door, turned toward the panopticon, and waved my arms over my head. I saw several of the eyes lock onto me immediately. To them, it looked like two guards — one waving and one unconscious on the floor. And for now, that was true.

It was barely two minutes before one of Krimm's trucks turned the corner onto my block. It pulled right up to the front door and two minions ran out while the driver waited behind the wheel.

"What happened?" one asked me.

I didn't want to answer in case they noticed the voice being different, so I just pointed at the body and at the kitchen. The guards were in such a hurry they barely took notice of me. They saw the blood on the ground and the oil spilled all over the kitchen, and decided it was too much work to clean up or help. After thinking for just a few seconds, he took a strange weapon out of his belt. It was gray and smaller than a brick, but I could barely see through the foggy lenses of my mask. He unfolded it once, so it doubled in length and extended it toward the man's head. It clicked with a sound no louder than a seatbelt, and I could tell that the man on the ground was now dead.

I couldn't react and risk giving myself away, so I watched in silence. I was grateful the mask hid my face, because I had no idea what it was doing currently.

"Come with us," the minion said and turned to walk back to the truck. He left the door open and gave no other instructions, so I turned and followed him to the truck. The other one who had gone to the house said nothing, just walked back to the truck behind me.

I was so nervous I felt like I'd throw up the entire trip to the tower. I would likely go into the mysterious building, and may even speak to Krimm himself. Would they interrogate me? Ask about the death of 'my partner'? What would I say?

6

We pulled up to the back of the building—the side on the opposite side from the glass door I'd tried to peer into before. There was a loading dock and port where the truck pulled into and we all got out. I walked with the men up and into the cargo doors, and expected them to take me to Krimm, or some other official who would review my situation.

Instead, they just walked in and spread out, each going to tend to his own duties, leaving me entirely alone, assuming I'd go about whatever it was I had to do. I stood in the middle of a bustling commotion of minions for a moment, waiting for someone to come and direct me to my debrief, but no one did. Each one seemed to be going about his own business, with no one caring about the expendable workers who now lay dead in my home.

When I realized no one was going to tell me what to do or where to go, I suddenly snapped into action, realizing that standing still would look more suspicious than walking with intent. I assumed a brisk pace, but also tried to look around and soak in the sight around me.

The innards of the tower were unrefined. In the middle of it was a massive opening which seemed to rise almost to the top of the tower. This surprised me that the inside of the building was nearly hollow. Around the edges of the building, on each level, was a walkway where minions paced constantly, each running to execute a duty or perform their function.

Along each of the walls ran those red cables which looked like veins or vessels of some sort. They were clearly the inputs from the eyes on the outside of the building, communicating somehow with the workers inside the building. There were so many of them it nearly felt like being inside a living, breathing organism. The walls were also pink and wet and seemingly alive, like the inside of a cheek.

I could not figure out how the eyes and the organs of the building communicated with the minions. How did they instantaneously know where to go and what to do? It felt so instant and thoughtless that it was more like instinct than a relayed, verbal message—like when you sense your hand nearing a hot stove and jerk it away without thinking. That's how the workers seemed to interact with the tower and all of its eyes.

I looked up the center of the building, where I could see up dozens of stories, and on each level I could see, the workers were running around, carrying out their various tasks, each set

on doing whatever they were assigned. There was no rest, no break areas, no sleeping mats. I wondered how they had the energy to be in constant motion with no rest or sleep. Surely they didn't go home and sleep—the fact that no one had left the building in plain clothes had been clearly reported.

But now here I was, an intruder in the building, undetected, and apparently, not on the same wavelength as these workers.

I walked over to a lift that went up as far as I could see, and waited by the door until the cart appeared. I stepped on with a few other workers. They all pushed a button for their floor, and I pushed the second from the top.

One of the others looked at me and simply said, "85?"

I looked at him and nodded and that was that.

The other guards. each got off at their respective floors and I rode it slowly up to the 85th floor. When it arrived, the fence slid open and I stood on a floor that was mostly empty. It was above the hollow area of the building, so the floor seemed to take up the entire breadth of the building. It was a mostly open floor with a high ceiling. On the far side of this lobby, straight across from the lift door, was an ornate looking double door.

To my right and left were tall windows. In any other building this would have seemed perfectly normal, but then I

remembered that I was in a building covered in eyes, which from the outside, had no visible windows whatsoever. How could there be windows from the inside but none visible on the outside? I didn't know, but couldn't think about it right now.

Two guards walked around the open lobby space, and both looked at me as the lift opened.

I had clearly come to Nephilous Krimm's office.

7

The two guards walked toward me. They weren't in a hurry, they seemed more to be coming over to hear a news update. I kept forgetting that I looked just like one of them now, and they couldn't tell I was an intruder. I also thought about how easily one of them had earlier killed one of his coworkers in my home, and knew I had to tread carefully or risk the same fate.

As they ambled over to me, I decided to confidently point at one of them, then point to the lift. He simply nodded and walked past me, onto the lift. He closed the gate and apparently knew exactly where to go, as I saw him pushing a button and going down. The other guard turned and walked back to resume his pacing around the grand lobby. I decided to try talking to him without betraying my identity.

"How is he today?" I asked.

The guard looked at me and said nothing and at first, I thought I had already given myself away. Then he shook his head and said, "Don't know. Haven't seen him yet."

"Should I go in and check on him then?" I asked. I wondered if my curiosity would eventually get me killed.

"Be my guest. Just don't forget what happened to Cyphil." Of course, I had no idea what had happened to Cyphil, and figured it would be better not to know.

I approached the large, ornate office doors and gave a courtesy knock as I pushed one open. I peeked my head in and looked at the man I'd been wondering about for over a year.

Nephilous Krimm stood looking out a window on the opposite side of the office, and I still had no idea how there were windows in this eye-covered building. He turned to look at me and gave me the same smile I'd seen him give the crowd months ago.

"Yes?" he said with a kind tone of voice.

"We — " I began, unsure of what to say. "We just haven't seen you all day and I wanted to be sure you're alright, sir."

His warm smile didn't change as he answered. "Yes, thank you for checking. But please never interrupt me uninvited again. This is your first and last warning," still with the unbroken smile.

"Yes, sir, I apologize," I said.

"No need to apologize, just don't let it happen again."

I turned to leave, disappointed that I didn't get any more insight about…any of this, when he said, "You must be one of the new ones, huh?"

"Uh, yes sir," I said, as it was not a lie.

"What's your name?" he asked. His smile seemed warm and sincere, but I also couldn't help but wonder if this was some sort of test.

"My old name?" I asked, totally guessing at what sort of answer he wanted, also guessing that they changed or lost names in this place.

"Good," he smiled again. "Just making sure."

I went to leave again when he said, "One last thing. Now that you're here, you've got me thinking…I could use some decompression. Come on up."

I had noticed a spiral staircase that went up to the ceiling, presumably to the 86th floor. That must be where he lives, in the penthouse. He turned to walk up the stairs and I didn't know what decompression meant, and I wasn't sure I wanted to know. It seemed like all the other workers were somewhat brainwashed and did whatever he wanted, and I didn't want to be another one. However, the combination of my curiosity and fear of what would happen if I resisted drove me to follow him up the stairs.

What I found was, unsurprisingly, the nicest apartment I'd ever seen.

Krimm led me up the stairs and through the kitchen, presumably to his bedroom, but I never found out. I apparently was going too slowly through the kitchen, looking around and soaking it all in, and he walked back toward me.

"Look," he said, with no more warmth in his tone. "Something has been off about you from the start. Do you need to go through orientation again?" Once again, I didn't want to know what orientation entailed.

"No sir," I replied.

He stared at me a second longer, then approached me and reached for my mask, to lift it up. But I grabbed his wrist. Quickly, without thinking, I pulled a small knife out of my belt with my other hand and rammed it under his armpit. He was so shocked it took a few seconds for him to react. He inhaled sharply, gasping for air. His eyes stared far away, and the strength slowly left his legs.

Nephilous Krimm began to say nonsensical things as he died. "With…hair? …Not on this…basket." He fell to his knees. Blood ran down his side and onto his pants.

I was somewhat shocked too.

I have no idea what drove me to pull the minion's knife from his belt and kill the most powerful man in the city, but it felt like the right thing to do. He had become too powerful and needed to be stopped.

My curiosity drove me to dig through Krimm's pockets and see what I could find. I still wanted to know so much more. But both his front pockets were empty, and then I noticed it. The chain of a necklace lay around his neck. It had risen up above his collar when he had fallen onto his side. I reached down and pulled it out of his shirt, and on the end was a jewel colored like I'd never seen before. It was a rich hue, and it wasn't just one color that could be described. As I rotated it, the hue changed. It was unbelievable.

I pulled it over his head and examined the jewel closer. Then I put it over my own head. And suddenly I saw.

in a way that transcends words, I could see everything. All the eyes of this massive building were somehow routed to my brain, and I could process and comprehend it all.

I saw my minions coming and going and I had perfect control of them all, the way a pianist has perfect, individual control of each of her fingers.

And I liked it.

the end

PUBLIC SERVICE ANNOUNCEMENT!

Friendly reminder that if you walk your beast from The Dimension, they MUST be on a chain. Please stop forgetting, or you and your pet will both be cast into The Dimension.

We are sorry again for all the pink and yellow. We know it's not pleasant.

Every day around 1:17,
I look out the window,
and see 'cross the street.
There's a man staring back,
or maybe a beast,
but it never moves,
or whispers, or blinks.

I don't want to see,
but I can't look away
from its multiple arms
and its towering frame.
Is it waving at me
or do my eyes just play tricks?
Does he come out and mess
with our heads just for kicks?

And I think I hear singing,
or crying aloud;
I can't quite make it out,
it's a harrowing sound.
Like a whistle, a wail,
or a song all at once.
Does it have any mouth?
Does it have any lungs?

All that I know is at 1:17,
my eyes are wide open,
it isn't a dream.
There's a man in the house
and he's all I can see;
I can't look away
because it looks just like me.

Animal Fact!

The Bugan (Latin: Scatus Containgus) is a rare creature only found in Crumb Hill. It cannot go to the bathroom on its own, so once a month, the Volunteer Bugan Draining Brigade (VBDB) goes around and empties them out.

Animal News!

It is with a heavy heart that we must announce that The Ape of the Lumber Field has gone to The Dimension today at 1:17. He will be missed. He was a good boy. He did a lot of good apework.

It's time for Crumbdog Millionaire! It's everyone's favorite game in Crumb Hill! To learn how to play, just look through the pictures and you'll quickly pick up the sequence of gameplay! We added some pointers, to make it crystal clear for the stupid. Have fun!

Warm up!

We cannot stress the importance of warming up your muscles before the intense gameplay of Crumbdog Millionaire, despite what Dr. Orvis says.

Make sure your Machine is in proper working order. Malfunctions are common. Begin gameplay at 1:17.

Consult The Oracle.

Summon Deborah.

If she plays with you, you greatly increase your chances of winning. If not, begin search for hair stew.

Half time!

It's important to observe half time seriously. You do *not* want to overdo it in this game. That is what has led to the ending of the careers of many a Crumbdog Millionaire.

It's important that you do not walk, stand, sit, whisper, breathe, or run during the half time intermission. The observance of the game's half time is of the utmost importance. Then, resume gameplay.

Endure public scorn.

We hope this was a helpful primer on how to play the town's favorite sport, Crumbdog Millionaire! Not only is it our favorite game, it's our oldest!

We believe that these cave drawings found in Crumb Cave show some of our ancestors engaged in a riveting round of gameplay.

You can tell it's Crumbdog Millionaire because of their interaction with the puck near the foul stalactite—they are clearly in round 43 of 117 due to the position of the wingbeast—and you can see The Oracle in the lower left.

We are sad to announce that we must ban all shady back alley deals. They have gotten out of hand. Deals must be made in the daylight and out in the open.

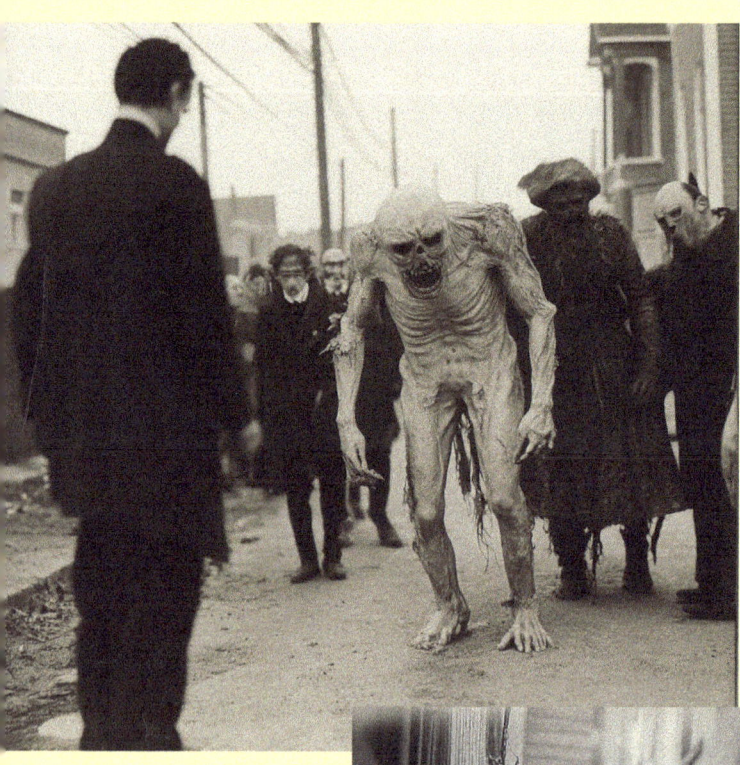

This is a Public Service Announcement by the way.

The Merryjack family, with their adopted son (far right).

Yarnfolk of Crumb Hill

Each year, the old ladies of Crumb Hill have a competition to see who can knit the best Yarnfolk and prompt him to life! Who do you think should win this year?

Her?

Her?

Her?

Her?

Her?

Crumbclusion
fine, leave…if you can.

We certainly hope you've enjoyed this cursory romp through our little town of Crumb Hill!

Were the stories illuminating and riveting?

Were the introductions to the various residents and their unique proclivities helpful?

Were you adequately warned about The Dimension?

Wasn't our prison so damp?

If not, then our Crumb Hill Office Of Tourism (CHOOT) will need to be reprimanded, firmly.

There is so much more we could say about our wonderful town. We love it here and we hope you come back often. If you can find it.

You may by now be wondering why our beloved town laureate Desmond Poots isn't writing this conclusion.

Well, that's because of a tragic Dimension accident that happened last night, and Desmond did not have proper Dimension Insurance.

We promise it was an accident. He went to toss a cat in, but slipped when he was near the entrance, and ended up falling in himself. He was not pushed. It was definitely an accident. Poor Desmond. Poor, poor Desmond.

Any other questions?

CRUMB

HILL

About the Historian

Compiling an history of a town is a unique project.

I have had to dig through old archives and learn numerous dialects of beastspeak. They often refused to open up until after hours of rubbing their big old bellies.

In order to prepare for this undertaking, I attended Moody Bible Institute for a degree in Communications, then Denver Seminary for a Masters in Theology. I also had to write ten previous books just to prepare for the monumental undertaking of writing the history and documentation for an entire town. Some titles are: *open hands, Bad Timing, All the Immortal Things that Live Inside of Us,* and *How to Understand the Entire Universe.* These are all available on the internet.

I also maintain a blog at www.ethanrenoe.com, where you can read not only about Crumb Hill, but many other wonderful things!

Follow Crumb Hill on Instagram at @crumbhill.

Follow the historian on everything at @ethanrenoe.

Thank you for reading this volume and we hope to continue to document the fascinating history of Crumb Hill for epochs to crumb!

—*Ethan Renoe*

www.ingramcontent.com/pod-product-compliance
Ingram Content Group UK Ltd.
Pitfield, Milton Keynes, MK11 3LW, UK
UKHW051432100925
7837UKWH00042B/674